Strange Tales from Strange Lands

Strange Tales from Strange Lands

Stories by Zheng Wanlong

Edited and with an Introduction by
Kam Louie

East Asia Program
Cornell University
Ithaca, New York 14853

The *Cornell East Asia Series* publishes manuscripts on a wide variety of scholarly topics pertaining to East Asia. Manuscripts are published on the basis of camera-ready copy provided by the volume author or editor.

Inquiries should be addressed to Editorial Board, Cornell East Asia Series, East Asia Program, Cornell University, 140 Uris Hall, Ithaca, New York 14853.

A slightly different version of the Introduction appears as "Masculinities and Minorities: Alienation in 'Strange Tales from Strange Lands' " in *The China Quarterly*, No. 132 (December 1992).

© 1993 by Kam Louie. All rights reserved
Printed in the United States of America
ISSN 1050-2955
ISBN 0-939657-85-6 cloth
ISBN 0-939657-66-X paper

Contents

Acknowledgments vii

Introduction 1

The Old Horse 23

Old Stick's Wine Shop 35

The Gorge 45

Yellow Smoke 59

Empty Mountain 69

The Wilderness Inn 81

The Earthenware Pot 89

Dog Head Gold 99

The Clock 113

Three-Tile Temple 123

Acknowledgments

I would like to thank the Key Centre for Asian Languages and Studies at The University of Queensland for a grant which facilitated the editorial and clerical process. I am most grateful to Alan Rix, Anne Platt, Kath Filmer, Lynne Schofield, Zhang Xiuqin and Chris Brassington for their generous support throughout.

The stories were translated by a group of students in my 1990 Honours class. Names of the individual translators appear at the beginning of each story.

A slightly different version of the "Introduction" appears as "Masculinities and Minorities: Alienation in 'Strange Tales from Strange Lands'" in *China Quarterly*, No.132, December 1992.

Introduction

The stories from "Strange Tales from Strange Lands" (*Yixiang yiwen*)[1] translated in this volume have often been used as typical examples of a literary movement in the mid-1980s known as "root-seeking literature" (*xungen wenxue*). Their author, Zheng Wanlong, has become one of the most celebrated writers in China, notably for his descriptions of the Oroqen minorities in China's northeast. For the Western reader, whatever the literary merits of these stories, there is no question that they provide a wealth of information regarding relations between the different racial groups in China as well as Chinese notions of masculinity and femininity.

In this Introduction, I will discuss the problematic relationship between depictions of primitivism and the search for essential Chineseness in the "Strange Tales." I will show that the dichotomous relationship between primitivism and Han civilization presented by Zheng reflects an alienated notion of essential Chineseness and human existence. Since Mao's death, Chinese intellectuals have expressed concern about the emergence of a "faith crisis" and described the younger generation as the "lost generation."[2] This Introduction will reveal that one stream of "root seeking" literature, in its attempts to mitigate the alienation or faith crisis within

---

1. There are altogether fourteen stories in this series. The first ten are "short stories" (*duanpian xiaoshuo*) and the remaining four are "medium-length stories" (*zhongpian xiaoshuo*). They have been identified by Zheng Wanlong himself as forming two distinct groups. See Zheng Wanlong, "Table of Contents," *Shengming de tuteng* (The Totems of Life) (Beijing: Zhongguo wenlian chuban gongsi, 1986). The first ten stories have been translated here.
2. See for example Li Honglin, "'*Xinyang weiji' shuomingle shenme?*" (What Does the 'Faith Crisis' Indicate?), *Renmin ribao* (People's Daily) (11 November 1980).

China that occurred during this period of increasing Westernization, has reflected and indeed perpetuated this very alienation.

The term alienation has a multitude of meanings and, as Raymond Williams has observed, these variable interpretations have often led to accusations of misuse and incorrectness. However, as Williams has argued, "it seems better to face the difficulties of the word.... In its evidence of [an] extensive feeling of division between *man* and *society*, [because] it is a crucial element in a very general structure of meanings."[3] There are three basic meanings for the process of estrangement that are instructive for our present analysis of the contemporary phenomenon "root-seeking literature." One of these is Rousseau's usage of the term to refer to the estrangement of people from their original nature. This has been understood as being either the estrangement of people from their historically "primitive" instinctive nature or their essential permanent nature. Alternatively, Freud regarded civilization as causing the alienation of people from their primal sexuality. The Hegelian and Marxian notions of alienation rejected concepts of estrangement from an original human nature, preferring instead to regard alienation as the process of objectification. Zheng Wanlong's "Strange Tales," in its attempt at revealing an essential selfhood, provides examples of each of these notions of alienation. In this Introduction I will point to the implications of this often contradictory and ambiguous demonstration of alienation by focussing on two major issues—sexual domination of women by men and racial domination of minorities by the Han. It will become evident that Zheng's tales propound a national and individual self, within terms of racial and sexual integration, that furthers an estranged vision of Chineseness and human existence.

Divided Roots

The "Strange Tales from Strange Lands" were originally published in the mid-1980s in literary journals such as *Beijing Literature* and *People's Literature*. Since then, they have become so popular that many have been selected for anthologies of contemporary fiction and the series, either as a whole or in part, has been reprinted in a number of book-length anthologies.[4] Zheng Wanlong himself has been hailed by critics as a

---

3. Raymond Williams, *Keywords: A Vocabulary of Culture and Society* (London: Fontana Press, 1976), p.36.
4. This includes a collection published in Taiwan. Bo Yang (ed), *Laobangzi jiuguan* (Old Stick's Wine Shop) (Taibei: Linbai chubanshe, 1988). At least one story from this series has been translated and published in English, see "Clock,"

foremost writer and his "Strange Lands" series has often been used in discussions on the *xungen* (root-seeking) school of writing.[5] This particular school was one of the most influential during the mid-1980s. But before analyzing the stories in terms of alienation, I will place them in the context of current intellectual concerns.

In the early 1980s, Chinese writers were able to experiment more freely than ever before under Communist Party rule.[6] The relaxation in censorship, coupled with the increased ease of international travel, created an environment within which a host of different schools of writing developed. No longer restricted to "realism," writers embraced an assortment of techniques, and called themselves or each other fashionable names such as symbolists, structuralists and absurdists.[7] The influence of Western ideas was of course not limited to the literary scene. In almost all disciplines, Chinese intellectuals were quickly assimilating and using ideas from abroad. For many, the pace of Westernization was too fast, and after the campaign against Spiritual Pollution of 1984, a backlash occurred. By the mid-1980s, the rediscovery and "inheritance" of Chinese tradition became a very fashionable intellectual pastime.[8] Conferences, books, journals and newsletters discussing "Chinese tradition" proliferated during this period.[9] In literature, one of the most important developments that

---

in Jeanne Tai (ed & trans), *Spring Bamboo: A Collection of Contemporary Short Stories* (New York: Random House, 1989), pp.5-18.
5. In 1986, *Beijing Literature* organized a special forum devoted specifically to the discussion of "Strange Tales from Strange Lands." A summary of the speeches made at this forum was later published in *Beijing wenxue* (No.3, 1986), pp.69-79.
6. I am referring here only to the official literature, that is, literature published by officially sanctioned publishers. In unofficial magazines and journals, experimentation thrived in the 1970s.
7. For example, starting from 1988, Wu Liang, Zhang Ping and Song Renfa have edited a series entitled "*Xin shiqi liupai xiaoshuo jingxuan congshu*" (A Series of Books on the Fiction of the Schools of the New Period) in which these schools are represented.
8. The concentration on China's cultural heritage is not unique to the post-Mao period. It was a major political issue almost as soon as the People's Republic was established. See Kam Louie, *Inheriting Tradition: Interpretations of the Classical Philosophers in Communist China 1949-1966* (New York: Oxford University Press, 1986).
9. Peking University, for example, established the International Academy of Chinese Culture in 1984. In the same year, The Chinese Academy of Social Sciences and Fudan University jointly published *Zhongguo wenhua* (Chinese Culture), a journal which is designed to revitalize the discussions on traditional Chinese culture.

reflected the general resurgence in interest in Chinese tradition was the appearance of "root seeking literature."

Xungen writers include some of the best authors in the contemporary Chinese literary scene, such as Ah Cheng, Han Shaogong and Jia Pingwa. Although the *xungen* writers wrote on very diverse subjects, they all seem to be preoccupied with mythologizing ancient or primitive settings as a means to reaching the "roots" of Chinese culture. The critics were aware that this was a common thread, but the "root seekers" only became a "school" when Han Shaogong published "The 'Roots' of Literature" in 1985. Here, Han claims that "Literature has roots. The roots of literature should be firmly buttressed in the soil of the nation's traditional culture."[10] This sentiment is clearly a reflection of the fears expressed by many that China was being overwhelmed by Westernization. In one of the concluding remarks in this manifesto, after Han Shaogong lists the momentous changes brought about by "taking" from the West, he reasserts the primacy of Chinese culture by claiming that

> China is still China. This is especially true in the areas of literature and arts, and in the nation's spiritual and cultural realms. We have the self of our nation, our task is to liberate the thermal energies of modern ideas and use them to recast and galvanize this self.[11]

While the exact nature of this "national self" is never clearly explained, the inclusion by Han Shaogong of writers from border regions such as Xinjiang, as well as his own area of Hunan, as examples of those who are discovering this "self," shows that it was not limited to Han Chinese. As the title of Zheng Wanlong's series suggests, the setting for this particular anthology is in "strange lands." In this case, it is in the Oroqen (or Elunchun) national minority areas of Heilongjiang.[12] From the search for a common root to Chinese culture, therefore, there emerged a root system which not only branched out into diverse parts, but fragmented the parts themselves. The "national self" includes a very disparate conglomerate of national minority selves which differed greatly from one another.

Ultimately, what Zheng Wanlong and his peers seek are their own personal roots. Born into a Han family in Heilongjiang in 1944, Zheng had

---

10. Han Shaogong, "*Wenxue de 'gen'*" (The 'Roots' of Literature), *Zuojia* (Writers) (1985, No.4), p.2.
11. Ibid, p.5.
12. The Oroqens are a very small national minority people living in the north-east of China. They engage mainly in hunting and mining. In the 1990 census, their numbers were only 6,965.

left his birthplace when he was only eight years old to attend school in Beijing, where he still resides today. As a consequence, unlike other *xungen* writers such as Han Shaogong and Jia Pingwa who have spent a considerable part of their adult lives in the villages they write about, Zheng Wanlong relies much more on "feelings" etched into his subconscious during his childhood.[13] This may explain why the settings for the stories seem strange and intangible, and are often shrouded in mist, smoke or snow.

In this paper, I will take the lead from Zheng Wanlong and treat his stories as traces of a dimly remembered past, to carry out an archaeological excavation of his memory by digging for clues and relics offered by these stories as a way to reconstruct the world vision of a typical *xungen* writer. By examining the ways in which Zheng Wanlong perceives human beings relate to each other and to their surroundings, I will show that the most important theme which runs through the series is one of alienation. Thus, while the narrator in each story may be telling a very personal experience, what emerges is not a sense of intimacy, but a world estranged, where men are men, women women, Chinese Chinese and savages savages.

Scripting the Macho Man

One of the main causes for this alienation is the concern with being a "real man" in a rapidly changing world.[14] Indeed, the first thing which strikes the reader on reading the "Strange Tales" series is their eulogy to machismo. Because the setting for the stories is in the harsh and savage landscape of the north-east, the heroes who thrive in this climate, like the frontiersmen in the adventures of the Jack London variety, must be men who could withstand any kind of challenge. Danger and violence are exciting and manly. Thus, in order to preserve his fame of fearlessness, Chen Sanjiao in "Old Stick's Wine Shop" would rather walk off into the snowbound hills with a fatal knife-wound than recuperate in the shop and live. And we are presented with men such as Shenken in "The Gorge," who dies embracing a bear he has just killed with a knife, because he refuses to

---

13. Zheng Wanlong, "*Wo de gen*" (My Roots), *Shanghai wenxue* (1985, No.5), p.44.
14. This concern is expressed in many forms, from the May Fourth intellectual type to the obedient Party soldiers of the Lei Feng variety. See Kam Louie & Louise Edwards, "Changing Masculinities in the People's Republic of China," unpublished paper.

use a gun on bears.[15] The men are also extremely callous in the way they treat sex and women, as illustrated by "the man's" treatment of Wurina in "Empty Mountain."

Again, while we are dealing with the writings of one man who is supposed to be telling us about strange customs of a strange land, Zheng Wanlong's fantasies in fact do not go beyond the standard "script" for the macho personality constellation described by the sexologists Mosher and Tomkins. This script invariably consists of "(1) the fight scene, (2) the danger scene, and (3) the callous sex scene."[16] These rituals are identified by Mosher and Tomkins as the rites of passage which enable a boy to become a "real man." While all the fourteen stories contain elements of these rituals, "The Gorge" in particular identifies the difference between boys and men.

In "The Gorge,"[17] two fourteen/fifteen year old boys, Bieerdan and Enduli, who are eager to prove that they are men, discover a bear in a cave. The bear is to be the trophy showing their manhood. But they are joined by a seasoned hunter, Shenken, who refuses to use a gun on the bear and dies embracing the bear, having killed it in a struggle with his knife. The story is a succession of stereotypical macho displays. Each scene is defined by values typical of the macho script. The locale for the action is in the frontiers, the actors are all men who dare, their quest is for domination and the unstated prize is initiation into manhood for the boys. The role of the hero in the story is to provide a "real man" model for the boys in defending to the death principles such as honour and tradition as well as winning the heart of a beautiful woman.

We could look at this story in terms of the three tests for manhood devised by Mosher and Tomkins. Firstly, there are several fight sequences in the text. As the men set out for the hunt, Shenken, baring his chest, taunts Enduli to shoot him. This bravado is naturally meant to be admired and modelled on by the boys. Shenken as model is later reinforced when he effortlessly disarms Enduli and Bieerdan who draw knives to fight the

---

15. The machismo displayed in these stories is again typical of many of the *xungen* writers. See discussion in Kam Louie, "The Macho Eunuch: The Politics of Masculinity in Jia Pingwa's 'Human Extremities'", *Modern China* (1991, Vol.17, No.2), pp.163-187.
16. Donald L. Mosher & Silvan S. Tomkins, "Scripting the Macho Man: Hypermasculine Socialization and Enculturation," *The Journal of Sex Research* (1988, Vol.25, No.1), pp.60-84.
17. Zheng Wanlong, "*Xiagu*" (The Gorge), in Zheng Wanlong, *Shengming de tuteng*, pp.25-40. From here on, quotations from the series will come from this collection.

older man. The fight scene between them is vividly portrayed, showing the skills of Shenken, "strong as a bear," wrestling and throwing the young men while chewing dried meat. The final fight scene, of course, is between Shenken and the bear. While both die in the struggle, Shenken dies protecting the two boys, thus earning their eternal respect and again establishing himself as a model for a "real man."

Secondly, the whole story, in a fashion typical of the series, is replete with impending danger and risk. Almost all the stories are concerned with killing and death. In "The Gorge," the challenge issued by Shenken when he bares his chest and dares the boys to shoot him is one ritual which is repeated in other stories. There is no reason why Shenken need risk this danger. In all the stories, danger is artificially generated by the "real men." In this particular instance, the overwhelming danger is created by Shenken, who insists on hunting the bear with knives only, on the grounds that bears are the totem for the Oroqen tribe. While this needless risk of life and limb seems to lack common sense, it is typical of the senseless macho behaviour of most heroes in the series. It is also part of the ritual for protecting principles such as honour and pride.

Finally, "The Gorge," like most of the other stories, has only male characters. Women do not appear at all. However, the physical absence of the women only accentuates their vital role in the macho posturings. Throughout the series, the men are described as squandering their earnings on prostitutes, fantasizing about women they have left behind, or having real or imagined sexual relations with other men's mothers, wives or daughters. Although actual sexual encounters between the men and women are rare in the series, the many sexual innuendoes found in nearly all the stories point neatly to the "callous sex" scene that is another prerequisite for macho manhood.

In "The Gorge," for example, Shenken asks the boys to deliver the "message" to the village beauty Wurina that she should no longer wait for him but marry someone else. The only evidence of intimacy between them is Shenken's claim that he had "stolen melons from Wurina." While Shenken's request may be seen as evidence of a romantic and lyrical streak in a rough and tough hunter, in the context of the series, it could also be seen as indicative of the callous relation men are supposed to have with women: "fuck 'em and forget 'em." In all the stories, the "real men" brag about the women who in most cases do not even appear on the scene. They delight in recounting to their mates details of women whom they have conquered and abandoned. As Mosher and Tomkins observe,

> To participate in these scenes in the presence of male friends or to recount these scenes in their presence bonds the male group together in a camaraderie of shared hypermasculinity.

Just as inclusion is a sign of "superiority," the exclusion of inferior males, females, and children attests to their inferiority. The social stratification into the strong or the weak has subsumed a sexual differentiation as strong *and* masculine or weak *and* feminine.[18]

The macho script, though described by American psychologists, is faithfully followed in these tales about strange lands in China. This suggests that in both cultures, the social stratification along sexual lines is seen as commonplace and true. What is significant about the uniformity with which these tales fit into the sex roles which seem standard even in American society, is that what is seen as common is prescribed as the norm. As R. W. Connell observes,

> if we distinguish what is normative from what is common, instead of blending them together, new and important questions emerge. It becomes possible to see what is 'normative' not as a definition of normality but as a definition of what the holders of social power wish to accept.[19]

The problem with living or describing a life according to a script and norms is that each actor is given prescribed roles to play. There is simply no room for the characters to express what is not already in the preconceived framework. All non-standard behaviour is considered deviant, and the framework of set roles conveniently eliminates other essential elements, such as power and class interest in a life totally lacking in imagination. In this case, it is a problem of imagining a life beyond a macho script. In Zheng Wanlong's strange tales, this possibility does not exist. All the characters have "scripted" roles which are highly conventionalized and predictable.

Zheng Wanlong's fantasy leads, therefore, to an alienated existence, where men have, in their machismo roles, no desire to be close to other men except as adversaries. Occasionally, the men in their hypermasculinity seem to share some kind of camaraderie when they talk about women or when they band together for sport or murder. However, this closeness and camaraderie of shared hypermasculinity is also an illusory one. In Zheng Wanlong's strange tales, that closeness inevitably breaks down.

Women

"Dog Head Gold" is a good example of the break-down of the

---

18. Mosher & Tomkins, pp.72-73.
19. R.W. Connell, *Gender & Power* (London: Allen & Unwin, 1987), p.52.

camaraderie under stress. The group of miners in this story, snowed in at the gold mines and deserted by the mining company, are slowly starving to death. These men have, before entering the mountains, sacrificed to the mountain gods and sworn allegiance in a manner similar to the traditional brotherhood ceremonies.[20] When the situation becomes hopeless, the relationship between the men understandably becomes extremely tense and hostile. The men begin to quarrel and attempt to dominate each other. What is interesting is that the pecking order is based almost entirely on gender. So if a man is seen to be more masculine, he is also considered to be more ruthless and powerful. Wang Jieshi, the strongest of all, bullies the men and dominates them. He also takes sadistic delight in molesting Slip Pants Li, a sixteen year old who had not quite joined the rank of "real men."

The sexual harassment endured by Slip Pants Li illustrates clearly how camaraderie depends upon all comrades having either the same masculine powers or a common enemy. In most cases, this is an enemy that the comrades can unite against. When one person looks effeminate and there is no common enemy to provide an outlet for aggression, the interaction changes, as in this passage:

> "Seeing you've bloody well grown up as good looking as this, your mother must have been really pretty." As soon as he had got under his quilt, Wang Jieshi had grabbed him. His eyes had burnt blue and he had snorted with laughter. He had pushed away from him and pulled up his trousers saying, "Don't you mention my mother!" Wang Jieshi had grabbed him again and held him even tighter. He had run his other hand roughly over the boy's face and body, sniggering. "I have never been with a woman. Feeling you up is just as good as feeling up your mother!" Then he had dragged him into an embrace against his chest...[21]

This sexual harassment of young men may be common among groups of men forcibly isolated from women such as those in prisons or labour gangs. The more feminine among the group can then become the butt of aggressive sexual transgression by desperate men attempting to reassert their individual beings through exhibitions of sexual power. In a Freudian sense, they are acts of men who try to salvage their alienated existence by trying to recover their libido. When the constant bragging of women they have left behind is no longer sufficient, they have to attempt to dominate other men

---

20. Zheng Wanlong, p.100.
21. Ibid, pp.93-94.

in a sexual manner. Unfortunately, as these stories indicate, such tactics never seem to bring about a satisfactory harmonious relationship. On the contrary, they expose the delicate and illusory nature of camaraderie: a state of affairs which only works so long as the power relations are accepted by all. But these attempts to break out from an estranged state by exhibitions of aggressive machismo only reveal a more complete, impersonal social network.

The clearest illustration of the use of the libido as a means for a temporal relief from an alienated existence is in the story "Old Horse." The events of this story are seen through the eyes of a small boy, whose Oedipal hatred of the Father's sadism towards his mother is the motif of this story, we are told very early on that

> If his mother hadn't called him, he definitely would have killed this...this filthy swine [the father]! Because at night, he also used the whip on his naked mother. Mother would only shed tears. She never dared to cry out loud.[22]

The father does this to punish Mother for having been romantically involved with a man who had since drowned. The man's aged horse is kept alive just so that the father can watch it suffer. Its condition is so weak that the father cannot maltreat it as he seems to do with his favourite horse, whipping it in the same way that he lashes his woman. In terms of feelings, both husband and wife seem as dead as the old horse. The sadomasochistic relationship between them only gives them occasional leases on life, when masochism is used as "essentially an attempt to escape from self, in the sense of achieving a loss of high-level self-awareness."[23]

The little boy in the story is obviously meant to represent the state of mind of the narrator/author. While alone, he is content to immerse himself in nature. The story begins with his musing upon the greatness of the universe as he looks at the evening sky. His personality is quite integrated here and needs no escape:

> The sun sank behind the mountain top. The grove of white willows along the river bank became an ashen blur, losing that clear edge that stirred people's hearts. The grasslands sank into a vast desolation, tranquil and chilling. Xiaoxiao sat on top of the haystack in front of the stable, lost in thought:

---

22. Ibid, p.3.
23. I am using the theory developed by Roy Baumeister here. Although he specifies this theory as being applicable to sexual masochism only at this stage, it seems to apply here as well. See Roy Baumeister, "Masochism as Escape from Self," *The Journal of Sex Research* (Vol.25, No.1, 1988), pp.28-29.

where do you separate day from night? At the top of the trees or behind the clouds?[24]

Very quickly, however, this lyrical mood is transformed into a violent one as the Father enters the story, and we witness the boy assimilating, against his will, the aggression and self-hatred of his parents. We also witness the disintegration of his oneness with the world. While he detests the man's world and believes that all men are insane, he would "pull out the hunting knife again and violently thrust it into the haystack."[25] At the same time, while he sympathizes with his mother, he looks at her wistfully, with an undercurrent of sexual desire, watching her "hang her head like a kitten, never even raising her head to look at the two men."[26] Thus, we have here again the modelling from role theory. This modelling, ostensibly carried out by the boy, is also for the reader. In all these stories,[27] the boys consciously or unconsciously try to assimilate as quickly as possible macho characteristics, the same characteristics which have caused the alienation in the adults. Caught unawares, the reader assumes the naivety of the boys and assimilates the same alienating values as well.

The division between men and boys is a very strict and distinct one. There are certain rites of passage which, once passed, make a boy a man. Thus, even though the distinction is clear, at least it is a matter of time before a boy becomes a man. The natural divide between men and women remains a gulf that, in Zheng Wanlong's stories, can never be bridged. In the case of men, there is at least the occasional attempt at some kind of interaction by the code of camaraderie. The interaction between men and women is either on a sadomasochistic level, in which each individual is only attempting to escape from his or her own miserable awareness, or when there is any possibility of intimacy between them, the man escapes by rejecting the woman.

There are many love scenes in these stories. But in almost every case, the men push the women away, to show, presumably, that as real men they can control their own desires whereas the women cannot. For example, in "Yellow Smoke" one of the rites of passage for the tribe is to risk death and walk into the smouldering mouth of the volcano. In order to do this, the protagonist, though engaged to the heroine, has to keep her at a distance.

---

24. Zheng Wanlong, p.1.
25. Ibid, p.3.
26. Ibid, p.4.
27. Another good example is the swaggering young boy Liu Santai in "Old Stick's Wineshop." By imitating the macho behaviour of the hero Chen Sanjiao, he is able to trample on the hapless Old Stick.

When she wants to sleep with him, he is horrified,

> "Mowa, do you want to destroy me?" Zhebie knocked her to the ground with his fist. "Our ancestors said that the god will not speak to men who have slept with a woman and that such men will never be able to return to the world again."[28]

In the end, both he and the woman are killed. Nobody wins, and the inseparable gulf is maintained. Once the men become real men and marry the women, of course, they can treat them in any way and regard them only as property that needs to be kept under lock and key. This is illustrated in "Old Horse" and "Wilderness Inn." In the latter story, the hero has an affair with his rival's wife. His rival is prepared to sell her to him, but he cannot afford to pay the price. However, the wife dies from maltreatment anyway. The steamy love-making scene after the woman is dead is worth quoting, to illustrate the interaction that is possible only between life and death. To keep to the code of keeping faith, the hero's loving feelings only emerge when the woman is dead, while all the time he is saying he should not have left her, but did anyway:

> As the fire burned, it became more vigorous and grew so warm that he took off his deer skin cape and bared his body... He removed Dazhenzi's clothes and shoes and spread the calico out flat on the *kang*. He held the warmed wine in both hands and painstakingly washed her body... She was so close to him. He could smell the warm odour of her body...[29]

While this scene is a very tender one, it is interrupted by the intrusion of the husband. The two men then talk about the unfinished business between them and the story ends with the husband shooting the lover dead. As Nelly Furman observes in her discussion of the relationship between woman and language, "in a world defined by man, the trouble with woman is that she is at once an object of desire and an object of exchange, valued on the one hand as a person in her own right, and on the other considered simply as a relational sign between men."[30] The woman is in a curious situation here, in that even when she is dead, she is both an object of desire and a medium of exchange between the two men. As in all the other stories, the woman's own wishes and life are neglected throughout the narrative.

Of course, in the stories, some women are more dominant than

---

28. Zheng Wanlong, p.49.
29. Ibid, p.78.
30. Nelly Furman, "The Politics of Language: Beyond the Gender Principle?", in Gayle Greene and Coppélia Kahn (ed), *Making a Difference: Feminist Literary Criticism* (New York: Methuen & Co, 1985), p.61.

others. The weakest women are the prostitutes who are bought by gold. These women, who are sexually available generally, are often referred to as "little widows" (*xiao guafu*). That is to say, they are available as commodities because they have in effect lost their owners, men who could support them and keep other men off. The objectification of the women, and hence of the men also, leads directly to the path of alienation.

As the critic Chen Mo points out, the women are treated very much like the gold in Zheng Wanlong's stories.[31] They are commodities to be sought, fought over and used like the rare nuggets in these icy lands. Most important, they are a means for the men to communicate, although this communication may be a fatal one. For example, in "The Old Horse," Father's purpose in living is to "punish" his dead rival through his wife; and the bond between the two rivals in "Wilderness Inn" is seen to be much stronger than that between them and the woman they are supposed to be fighting over. For the Oroqens, the women are evil forces coming between the men and the mountain god, as illustrated in "The Clock." As commodities and media of exchange, the women in Zheng Wanlong's stories do not themselves establish any kind of links. There is no mention of friendship or interaction between women in these tales of manly exploits. The only time when an interaction between two women is portrayed is when the mother locks her daughter out of the hut in order to make her run away when they are being hunted. They both get killed and sacrificed. The tribe sees them as witches. Their fate serves the double function of warning the reader about women who are not alienated from each other, and also about the barbarity of primitive national minorities.

Oroqen Alienation

Here we can turn to another common perception of alienation: Rousseau's idea that man, by a process of civilization, is estranged from his original nature, that is, from himself. The Oroqens in Zheng Wanlong's stories tell us a lot about how this problem is supposed to be resolved. Thus, critics such as Cai Xiang claim that compared to the civilized world, people who live in barbaric worlds such as those in "Strange Tales" still possess a certain daring. They love more thoroughly and exclusively than

---

31. Chen Mo, "*Qian tan 'Yixiang yiwen' de bu zu*" (A Brief Talk on the Deficiencies of 'Strange Tales from Strange Lands'), *Beijing wenxue* (1986, No.3), p.73.

the civilized do, and they possess a passion the city dwellers have lost.[32] I will attempt to show that this is just more fantasy.

While the women in the strange tales have been categorized into commodities and media of exchange, the Oroqens as a whole seem to undergo rituals and rites which deprive them of even that objectified worth. Their feelings are described as codified and ritualized to such an extent that any "daring" or "passion" that deviates from the norm is quickly eliminated by the tribe. The ritualistic behaviour of the Oroqens which seems to rob them of individual human feelings is most clearly illustrated in the story "The Clock" because it is here that a direct contrast is made between the Hans and the Oroqens. We are told here that when the hunting and food gathering of the tribe gets tough, they blame the daughter of a "witch" who has jinxed both her parents-in-law and husband. Because this woman's men have died on her, people in the tribe blame her for all the natural calamities that befall the tribe, and when the protagonist falls in love with her daughter at a time of shortage, he too is hounded and nearly killed. He runs away and the two women, the younger pregnant, are sacrificed to the mountain gods. As could happen with magical rites, the tribe is again able to hunt fruitfully. This contrasts with "Yellow Smoke" where the magical practice of walking into the volcano may or may not help the tribe. Stories such as these show, in the cold light of the Han reader, how superstitious the Oroqens are. Their rituals are empty.

In "The Clock," the ostensible simplicity of the primitive is clearly shown when the wounded protagonist is rescued by a Han person. The Oroqen does not trust his saviour, to the extent that when told that the monster hanging on the wall tells the time, he feels cheated and cannot understand how a little devil with two running hands can tell the time. In the end, the ticking of the clock drives him crazy and he goes back to his tribe to find his lover and her mother sacrificed, and their corpses covered with animal intestines, food for the swarm of flies. Beneath this grissly spectacle, his tribespeople are having a feast after a successful hunt.

Whether Oroqens still perform these primitive rituals is irrelevant, and even if they do, it is unlikely that Zheng Wanlong would have witnessed them. What is fascinating about the whole series of stories about these primitive people is that they are the prototypical "Other." Much more than the women in the stories, there is never any meeting ground between the Hans and the Oroqens. Even when young progressive Oroqens are described

---

32. Cai Xiang, "*Yeman yu wenming: pipan yu zhangyang*" (Barbarism and Civilization: Criticism and Praise), *Dangdai wenyi sichao* (Contemporary Literary and Artistic Currents) (1986, No.3), p.76.

wanting to earn money from the Hans or copy their ways, or wanting to travel to the cities to learn, they are spurned. And "The Clock" shows that even if the Oroqens are living in the homes of the Hans, they can never understand them. In racial terms, this is estrangement of the most fundamental kind. It seems in these stories that the Han are Han and minorities minorities and never the twain shall meet. For many of the *xungen* writers who found the ways of life in border areas bizarre and incomprehensible, primitivism is often used as an excuse to explain their own inability to integrate with the locals when they settled in these areas.

As most of the writing about the segregation between the Hans and minorities is taken from the Han, or dominant racial group's, point of view, we can only conjecture whether the racial estrangement felt by the Hans is actually reciprocated. What we can say fairly definitely, however, is that if "Strange Tales" is taken as a typical case, then the Hans certainly feel alienated from their compatriots. The story "My Light" deals with the Han-Oroqen interaction on a symbolic level. It depicts fairly well the tensions and impossibilities of understanding between the two racial groups.

The story is about Han groups being led by Oroqens into the virgin lands to investigate the possibilities of establishing a tourist base. Throughout the story, there is conflict between the Hans and the Oroqen father-son guides. Furthermore, there also seems to be a generational conflict between the father and the son, with the son more prepared to sacrifice their sacred land for the possibility of wealth coming into the region. But at the end of the story, when the setting sun on the silhouette of a sacred mountain is reflected in the lake and father and son see the reflection as the rising of a god-like horse, they both break into incomprehensible chants which puzzle even the old professor who is quite prepared to be understanding. In the end, by concentrating his gaze through his camera lens and not watching where he is going, the professor falls to his death; a peaceful one, we are told. Notwithstanding the insistence by the Oroqens that this Han professor, with his death, becomes an honorary Oroqen, the message of the story clearly tells of the segregated existence of the two groups.

In a similar vein, the story "The Base of a Western Bottle" tells of the estranged existence of the Hans, who are the primitives now, and some "yellow hairs" from Harbin who hire the Han guides in their mining expeditions. The young man, Sangui, does not want their paper money, but is fascinated by the glass from the bottom of their wine bottle which filters a world of blue. This bottle is smashed and scorched. Later, the son kills (or knocks unconscious) the wine-shop owner and takes twenty bottles of the alcohol, smashing every one of them. In the end, he is still fascinated with the original, burnt one:

He then understood. He took out from his bosom that piece of burnt bottle base, covered completely with cracks. He looked through it everywhere. Wherever he looked, that place was cracked. The sun, like a fireball, was also cracked. Perhaps the world is like this.[33]

In terms of race relations, these stories reveal a world that is surely "cracked."

Part of the problem with these stories is that they are about primitives written by an intellectual in Beijing. They are categorized by a city mind and the categories are very much the dichotomy between Oroqen-Han or its corresponding country-city. Whatever the origins and influences which make up Zheng Wanlong's literary landscape, its popularity and typicality certainly point to a common conception among the reading public of what humanity in the wild, stripped of its city gloss, should look like.

By accepting Zheng Wanlong's Oroqens as the archetypal natives, readers and critics agree with the author's stated intention that he is displaying the manifestations of original human nature in the wild.[34] It is interesting to see that this original human nature is seen to possess still the "human passions" which culture has swamped or diluted. At the same time, it seems unlikely that any readers would really want to return to the wild passions of the savage. It is only an Other, to be conjured up when describing behaviour which is laughably naive or obviously sadistic and violent.

Faith and Illusion

The characters in these stories, whether they be men, women or children of whatever racial group, emerge as leading lives that are alienated from each other. When critics say that, unlike urban dwellers, the people depicted in these stories are true to themselves, the implication is that somehow, they remain faithful to their own beliefs, whether belief in a god or a value system peculiar to them. The values and moral code which dominate the strange tales can in fact be summed up in the traditional concept of "keeping faith" (*zhong* or *yi*). It is used to dignify certain forms of behaviour which in a more "civilized" context would be considered the height of stupidity. Thus, in "Empty Mountain," Grandfather dies by

---

33. Zheng Wanlong, p.172.
34. See for example the discussion in Li Shulei, "*Cong 'xunmeng' dao 'xungen'*" (From 'Seeking Dreams' to 'Seeking Roots'), *Dangdai wenyi sichao* (Contemporary Literary Currents) (1986, No. 2), p.47.

walking into a huge bonfire of logs which he has guarded for nearly twenty years, all the time keeping faith that the logging company would return to collect them; and in "Three-Tile Temple," the husband and wife freeze to death because they continue to have faith in the sacrificial rites to the mountain god, despite evidence pointing to the futility of such rites. In these stories, the people are rarely rewarded for their faith, and their unquestioning adherence to such faiths, instead of leading them to fulfilling lives, more often than not turns them into isolated beings completely alienated from everybody and everything around them.

The fates of both Grandfather in "Empty Mountain" and the couple in "Three-Tile Temple" suggest that for all their faith, the people in these stories are labouring under an illusion. This is true for every aspect of their lives, including the justifications they give for living. Thus, for the Han men in this region, the major preoccupation is to find gold. However, as "Dog Head Gold" indicates, even when they find a big nugget, it turns out to be fools' gold. In the process of discovering this, the men are literally driven mad or to their deaths. For the Oroqen men, the major preoccupation is to devise ways of taming nature, and they have created Bainaqia, the mountain god, as a means to this end. Again, in almost every case, the illusory Bainaqia is completely indifferent to the cruelty and sorrow generated in its name. Through their adherence to this illusion, their estrangement from the misery and self-destructiveness of their concrete conditions, and the hollowness of those who praise this spirituality, becomes apparent.

In a critique of the three stories "The Earthenware Pot," "Dog Head Gold" and "The Clock," Huang Ziping suggests that Zheng Wanlong is very Buddhist/Daoist in his attitude towards human life. He observes that Zheng Wanlong seems to have followed the formula "X+0=0" in concluding his stories.[35] That is to say, no matter what the subject matter, the story ends up saying that the pursuit for a meaning in life comes to naught. In "The Earthenware Pot," for example, the people suspect that the pot is full of gold, or at least contains some sentimental keep-sake, because Zhao Laozi guards it jealously all his life. The story describes him jumping perilously into a river of fast-flowing icebergs to retrieve this pot. Miraculously, he survives and to everyone's amazement, they learn the pot is empty. This Buddhist/Daoist twist is echoed in the writings of the other *xungen* writers,

---

35. Huang Ziping, "*Zheng Wanlong de 'tao guan,' 'goutou jin,' he 'zhong'*" (Zheng Wanlong's 'Porcelain Tin,' 'Dog Head Gold' and 'The Clock'), *Beijing wenxue* (1985, No.12), p.70.

Ah Cheng in particular.[36]

Apart from a philosophical attitude, however, there is little else Daoist or Buddhist about characters who inhabit Zheng Wanlong's "strange lands." The extreme jealousies and sadistic violence of Father in "The Old Horse" and the protagonists in "The Wilderness Inn" represent the worst of human foibles seen in a Buddhist/Daoist light. The religious attitude that is supposed to come through seems instead to be more a primitive shamanist one. The "0" which Huang Ziping points to seems to reveal a nihilistic and fatalistic attitude towards human existence. Certainly, in "Yellow Smoke" and "The Clock," any people who question "Tradition," as represented by the words of the shamans, are destroyed by their own tribes. Furthermore, being resigned to one's fate is a very Confucian virtue. Mencius admonished that "though nothing happens that is not due to destiny, one accepts willingly only what is one's proper destiny."[37]

This Confucian fatalism is typical of much of post-Mao fiction. There is undoubtedly a strong sense of futility which pervades the early stories by former "educated youth," who make up the bulk of the *xungen* writers.[38] In his history of realism in modern Chinese literature, Wen Rumian suggests that *xungen* writing began in the 1940s after Mao Zedong's Yan'an talks in which writers were urged to go into the villages and learn from the masses.[39] While there are some similarities between the "educated youth" writers and those who had lived amongst the peasantry in the 1940s and who wrote about their experiences, the two kinds of literature which have emerged cannot in fact be more different. The fatalism which typifies the "Strange Tales" is completely absent in the earlier works.

Fatalism in this case implies an acceptance of whatever life has to offer. In the China of the 1980s, when there was supposed to be a widespread crisis of faith, fatalism was tantamount to accepting an alienated existence. While Zheng Wanlong's vision is limited and alienating, for the Chinese reader of the mid-1980s, who has been used to a horizon of an even more limited variety, the "Strange Lands," with its exotic landscape and

---

36. For a discussion of Ah Cheng's relationship to Daoism, see Kam Louie, "The Short Stories of Ah Cheng: Daoism, Confucianism and Life," *Between Fact and Fiction: Essays On Post-Mao Chinese Literature and Society* (Sydney: Wild Peony, 1989), pp.76-90.
37. *Mencius*, D. C. Lau (trans & introd) (Harmondsworth: Penguin Books, 1979), p.183.
38. See Kam Louie, "Educated Youth Literature: Self-Discovery in the Chinese Villages," in *Between Fact and Fiction*, pp.91-102.
39. Wen Rumian, *Xin wenxue xianshizhuyi de liubian* (Changes in Realism in the New Literature) (Beijing: Beijing daxue chubanshe, 1988), pp.185-196.

unusual practices, came as a brave new development in fiction writing.[40] The stories are a welcome respite from a literature which mostly dealt with the "normal" concerns of the civilized in urban China. Nevertheless, it is the attitudes expressed in these stories which seem to have struck a chord in the reading public. In the mid-1980s, fatalism still reigned supreme.

Totemism and Alienation

People are often fatalistic when they have no control over their own lives. Ritualistic adherence to fatalistic beliefs emerges from within particular social frameworks. According to Erving Goffman, human interaction is "framed" by social definitions which give the behaviour a specific contextual meaning.[41] While it is not always easy to analyze these frames to arrive at the social definitions, there is always the danger that these frames are rigidly adhered to, so that the problems connected with role modelling are again raised. While Zheng Wanlong's stories, like all writing coming out of China, should be looked at in context, it seems also true that the values these contexts have confronted are also universal and fit any social formation. If the values and morality which are fixed in Zheng Wanlong's tales are frames, these frames seem to be little different from the ones we have of the macho world in the West, or, for that matter, the macho world of Han China. What he has provided for us, of course, is not only the separate existence of men and women, but the tension between Hans and minorities. All these groups of people, either as groups or as individuals, seem to be completely estranged from one another and from themselves.

This state of alienation from oneself and others can be interpreted in a variety of ways. As we mentioned above, alienation can be seen in a Hegelian/Marxist light. The Hegelian/Marxist dialectic sees man's nature as being shaped by himself as well as by external factors. In the process, he has objectified himself and others and becomes alienated. In order to overcome this kind of alienation, man would have to transcend the objectification process. He does this by recovering the human powers he has surrendered to an alienating God, or ending the class society which

---

40. Male-centred vision is definitely not peculiar to the Chinese. Thus, American Sinologists such as Leo Lee have urged that works from the *xungen* genre be treasured, seeing them as bamboo sprouts shooting up after a period of literary and artistic repression, sprouts which "may yet mature into magnificent stands of literary masterworks." Leo Oufan Lee, "Introduction," in Jeanne Tai, p.xvii.
41. Erving Goffman, *Frame Analysis: An Essay on the Organization of Experience* (New York: Harper & Row, 1974).

divides people from each other and alienates them from their own labour.

It can also be argued, as some critics do, that Zheng Wanlong's Oroqens may not be integrated as far as relations with people are concerned, but that they are in tune with Nature; that alienation only applies to the civilized Han, not the noble savage. This interpretation of alienation, in which man is seen as cut off from his original nature, has its origins in Rousseau, and many thinkers have tried to devise ways to regain this lost original nature. For example, Freudians saw the recovery of libido or sexuality as a way back to the original and integrated human being. For men, this libido is perceived to be closely connected with being well adjusted with a certain masculinity.

No matter which sense of the word "alienation" we choose, however, the discussion above shows that the characters in Zheng Wanlong's stories are alienated: we have seen the Freudian use of the recovery of libido as leading, not to an integrated being, but to sado-masochism; we have seen Rousseau's primitivism as leading, not to any nobility of the savage, but to senseless savagery; and we have seen the Hegelian/Marxian use of the transcendence of objectification as leading, not to oneness with God or other human beings, but back to superstition or gender/race oppression. So, for Zheng Wanlong, all these methods have failed.

Why this failure? A clue to an answer to this question lies in the title of one anthology of these stories, *The Totems of Life*. Totemism has often been used as a symbol for the strange and incomprehensible in primitive societies. Zheng Wanlong's stories also evoke in his readers the feeling of hearing "cries from a primitive wilderness."[42] As Lévi-Strauss observes,

> By the bizarre character attributed to it, and which was further exaggerated by the interpretations of ethnographers and the speculations of theorists, totemism served for a time to strengthen the case of those who tried to separate primitive institutions from our own.[43]

Lévi-Strauss has shown, however, that "the term totemism covers relations, posed ideologically, between two series, one *natural*, the other *cultural*."[44] Furthermore, totemism is primarily concerned with the

---

42. Wang Bin, Zhao Xiaoming, "*Dangdai shenhua: 'tengtu' de shuailuo*" (Contemporary Myths: The Decline of 'Totems'"), *Xiaoshuo pinglun* (Xian) (Fiction Criticism), No. 2, 1988, p.9.
43. Claude Lévi-Strauss, *Totemism* (Harmondsworth, Penguin Books, 1969), p.176.
44. Ibid, p.84.

transformations and permutations between levels in formal systems, which followed a logic whose form was universal, however much its particular manifestations varied from culture to culture. This logic from one aspect was a continual search for difference, establishing oppositions by the application of a basic principle. Thus, the dichotomies nature/culture can be seen as repeated in the opposition between, for example, hunting bears with knives for food (natural) and hunting bears with guns for fun (altered by culture). In the case of the Oroqens, this relationship is masked by the bear having a totemic stature within the tribe, so that Shenken for example calls the hunted animal "uncle."

Totemism is therefore really about naming and relationships between different categories. However, there is nothing very primitive or bizarre about either naming or correspondences between the name and the function. Confucius, after all, had decreed, "Let the ruler be a ruler, the subject a subject; the father a father, the son a son."[45] He was adamant that the ills of the world at his time were due to a neglect of the proper observance of the moral order of the day, that men used and abused their positions in the universe by not paying attention to the correct rituals they should perform.

An insistence on the correct observance of formal rituals is as old as culture itself. In China, the idea that there is a rigid correspondence between the name of a thing and its relationship to other things was already made orthodox when Confucius had used the rectification of names as a weapon against the Daoists who were much more fluid in their conception of the relationship between things, their names and their functions. The *Daodejing*, after all, begins with "The way that can be spoken of is not the constant way; the name that can be named is not the constant name."[46] The Confucian rectification of names, as many scholars have already pointed out, is really for the subjugation of those who are named as lowly. Worse still, in terms of groups of people, it prevents any attempt at interaction between different categories. As the *Totems of Life* insists, any transgressions, for example, killing the totemic bear with guns, would bring disaster to the tribe.

However, as Lévi-Strauss' work on totemism has indicated, totemism is more than just the concrete manifestations of what ultimately resides in people's minds. Totemism is about categorizing the universe. While the modern man's fear of moral chaos and "spiritual pollution" is answered

---

45. *Confucius: The Analects*, D. C. Lau (trans & introd) (Harmondsworth: Penguin Books, 1979), p.114.
46. *Lao Tzu: Tao Te Ching*, D. C. Lau (trans & introd) (Harmondsworth: Penguin Books, 1963), p.57.

precisely by this totemism of the primitive mind, the problem with totemic classifications is that they "seem to be there to divide men up from each other."[47] The world described in the "Strange Lands" is a "man's world": it is rough, tough and hostile. Most of all, its inhabitants seem incapable of escaping a state of constant alienation which has been imposed on them by the roles they are meant to perform in a predetermined script.

---

47. Roger C. Poole, "Introduction," in Claude Lévi-Strauss, *Totemism*, p.62.

The Old Horse
Translated by T. Nelson

The sun sank behind the mountain top. The grove of white willows along the river bank became an ashen blur, losing that clear edge that stirred people's hearts. The grasslands sank into a vast desolation, silent and chilling. Xiaoxiao sat on top of the haystack in front of the stable, lost in thought: where do you separate day from night? At the top of the trees or behind the clouds?

Father returned, with the team of horses. At the very back of the team was an old horse; so old that one breath of wind could topple it. It walked swaying from side to side, with two men supporting it as if it were an old woman. The horses weren't in the yard; they were all outside, tethered to the trough. A large swarm of midges, brought back with them from the grasslands, clouded around the lantern like smoke.

Father's horse, the chestnut coloured Dun River horse he had bought from a Russian, was suspended from the wooden roof beams at the gate to the corral. The reins were pulled to breaking point and the horse's entire head was raised upwards like the spout of a kettle. Its two front hooves could only just touch the ground and the muscles on its chest were trembling as if they were about to rip apart. Tonight, again, Father did not let it eat. In the process of trying to tame the horse he had beaten it and had broken several oak poles as wide as the top of a bowl. He had dislocated his leg and for a fortnight he couldn't move from his *kang*. He and the horse had become bitter enemies and now almost every day he cruelly tormented it.

Mother, along with many other people, tried to persuade him to stop. He would always retort, "If I don't torment it to death, it will torment me to death. That's life, damn it." Xiaoxiao didn't understand what this meant, but he hated the way the old man treated the horses.

Behind the herd of horses was a luxuriant forest of willows. Xiaoxiao watched the pallid gold crescent moon obliquely hanging there, shrouded in a layer of icy air. When the wind blew it seemed to rock like a small boat. Beneath was an expanse of springs of all sizes, and frogs croaking their busy chorus.

In the moonlight, the two storey building, *Mukeleng*, which was surrounded by yellow pineapple plants and situated in the threshing ground, glistened with a nebulous but dazzling white light.

"Aiyee—! Aiyee—!," Father called to the dogs in his usual bellowing manner.

Xiaoxiao didn't need to run over and look. He already knew the size of the piece of raw mutton, dripping with blood, that Father held in his hand. The dogs barked madly. Even the longhaired sheepdog went to be fed. The family used to have two such longhaired dogs but the male one had died. Father had killed him. Since the male dog died the bitch had never barked. She made only a whimpering sound, like the low whistle of the cold wind sweeping through the branches of the trees.

Xiaoxiao liked Father's resonant voice. He liked the bright spots and sweat on his face after a day's working on the grasslands. He also liked the big beard with grass seeds stuck in it. However, Xiaoxiao didn't like the pair of slightly protruding eyes or the gaze that burnt like fire when he stared at the dogs as they ripped the mutton apart. Every day, when Father, mean fellow that he was, returned from the plains, he would toss a large piece of mutton to the pack of dogs with a "Hey," and watch greedily as they would snatch at it, chase it, pounce on it and then tear it apart. Sometimes, his eyes bright, he would laugh silently until the tears flowed down his cheeks.

Xiaoxiao didn't understand; why was his father like this? Xiaoxiao had watched him once, when he discovered the longhaired dog snatching a piece of mutton and running to hide behind the mill. He caught it with a pole that they used to harness horses with. Tying its front legs together he hung it from a wooden rack—the one they used for administering medicine to the horses. Its head was several yards from the ground and its two hind legs struggled as though it was paddling water. It barked twice and moaned, so that it sounded as though it was dying. The sound seemed to come from a far and distant place. Father took off all his clothes, and without uttering a sound he took a long horse-whip and thrashed the longhaired dog. Strip after strip, the dog's skin exploded open, flesh and blood binding itself around the whip and splattering onto the wooden rack. The blood and flesh also splashed onto the hot and sweaty body of that cruel swine who was his Father. The dog had already been whipped to shreds but that whip still kept cracking. Stroke by stroke, the whip crunched into its flesh. That swine's eyes bulged and flashed like the blue light in a jack-o-lantern. He was enjoying it.

Xiaoxiao hated his Father, this swine, intensely... Listen, he's beating that longhaired dog again... Xiaoxiao ran a few steps and stopped to gaze at that jet-black back covered in beads of sweat. Snatching the hunting knife from his waist, he walked quietly over to his father.

"Xiaoxiao—! Xiaoxiao—! Where are you?... Quickly, come and have dinner," Mother called him.

If his mother hadn't called him, he definitely would have killed this...this filthy swine! Because at night, he also used the whip on his naked mother. Mother would always only shed tears. She never dared to cry out loud.

Was this a man's world? If so, then all men were insane. I am a man too, Xiaoxiao thought. Will I also be like this when I grow up?... He pulled out the hunting knife again and violently thrust it into the haystack. He watched the blade shining, reflecting a cold light onto the stalks of straw.

The evening wind came down. From the top of the Daxing'an Mountains it brought a strong, sweet odor of wild pears and mountain berry wine, which spread over the entire Tartar grasslands. Above, the crescent moon tilted drunkenly. Only at this time of night could you hear the crashing sound of the Heilong River. It was like putting your ear to the belly of a horse. It rumbled and rolled, heavy and far away, as though there were another world in there.

Father came to see his horse. He held the lantern very high, close above the horse's ears, where it darted back and forth like a flame. He stopped in front of the old horse and for a long time he stood there mumbling to himself and lightly stroked the horse's nose. But he didn't look at the Dun River horse, nor did he look at Xiaoxiao. He didn't like Xiaoxiao. Even when he saw him he didn't say a word. They very rarely spoke to each other.

From a distance, Xiaoxiao could smell the warm and bitter odor of sweat on Father's body. It smelt like paste made from horseteeth grass or the smell of a handful of snowflakes.

"Xiaoxiao—! Xiaoxiao—! Where are you?... Quickly, come and have dinner!" Mother always called him like this, just as if she was calling a dog.

She was really a meek woman. Every time they had dinner she would sit on the stool by the door and silently drink her sour milk. Even when she chewed pickled cabbage she didn't make a sound. He didn't know why she loved to drink sour milk so much. She could drink a whole pint at once. She would hang her neck like a kitten, not even raising her head to look at the two men.

Xiaoxiao liked the exposed snow-white nape of her neck. It had a soft and smooth, milky lustre. He considered her the most beautiful woman in the world. When she was younger she must have been even more beautiful. Some day, he wanted to find a woman like this.

That bastard, on the other hand, ate like a pig—wheezing and belching. He grasped the leg of mutton with both hands and it struggled like a hunted animal in his hands. His muscles were like rolling stones. Frequently, he would wipe the oil from his hands on to the front of his gown, and pick up the copper bowl with both hands and gulp down the wine. He drank until his eyes became as red as the blood-filled eyes of a murdered bear.

As soon as Xiaoxiao saw those eyes he would not feel like eating. His mother had told him many times: "Your father hasn't had an easy life. It wasn't here that your grandfather settled down and made a living. It was at E'ergunei River, panning for gold. There was a fight then over a nugget of 'Dog Head Gold'. Your grandfather died and your father set fire to the shanty. That very night he stole over ten horses and fled here to this grassy marshland. When he first arrived there weren't so many trees or so much grass. The whole area was covered in springs..."

But did any of this make a difference to Xiaoxiao? He was already grown up. He could never forgive his father for what happened during the nights, or for the death of the longhaired dog. He couldn't forgive those eyes.

As usual, he came and sat on the top of the haystack. Every night it was the same: he would keep watch in the moonlight and by the light the lantern over the horses eating the hay. He could call out each horse's name, but he preferred the sound of them chewing hay. Hearing it felt like two soft hands gently stroking him. He firmly believed that in this world there were many, many invisible things. Otherwise, to whom was mother talking when she stood in front of those three incense sticks before going to bed every night?

Father had more than two hundred horses, though they weren't like the young horses he once had. There was no one in this area who could compare with him. Other horse owners didn't give their horses anything to eat at night. They only grazed their horses during the day. However, not only did Father feed his horses hay at night, he also added fried beans or bean cakes to the hay. He even opened an oil extraction mill especially for this purpose. Mother said that the oil extraction business made lots of money, but she also said that a lot of money was of no use. Xiaoxiao agreed that money was useless. He had grown this big and had never spent any money. Everything here was bartered for.

Every day Xiaoxiao would sit on the haystack and eat fried beans. The beans were very tasty. He would grab a handful from the horse's trough and stuff them one by one into his mouth until it was full of the delicious flavor. It was great to sit there chewing beans with the horses.

All the horses knew him. They would rub their noses up against him and snort.

The old horse was at the furthest end of the trough. The lantern hanging from the roof beam wasn't there to light up the hay for it to eat, but to attract mosquitoes and insects.

Those horrible little insects would constantly sting the horse's eyes. Like yellow muddy soup, opaque tears would flow endlessly from the corner of its eyes. It was old, so old it was ugly. All its bones showed through its skin. Except for its spirit, all that was left was its skeleton. Its teeth were all broken so it could no longer chew beans. The hair around its mouth had turned white and it swayed to and fro as it walked. But Father looked after this horse extremely well, not the way he treated the Dun River horse or the longhaired dog. He was full of sincerity and seriousness and other emotions that were hard for other people to comprehend. As soon as he saw the old horse his eyes would change; they would become dim and dull. He hired two men especially to wait on this horse because it could no longer go with the other horses to graze. After walking for a short while it would have to lie down, and after lying down it needed two men to help it back up. They kept watch by its side—inseparable as body and shadow—for fear that after the horse fell over it wouldn't get up again. When the horse arrived back at the trough, the men kept it upright with four poles and supported it from underneath with two belts. It was like torture. Even if it had wanted to fall it couldn't.

Xiaoxiao didn't understand why father kept the horse like this. One day he asked him: "Why don't you kill it?"

"Kill it?... You bastard!"

"It must be awful for it to go on living like this...those two workers said it would leave behind a good hide."

"I don't need one."

"Sooner or later it's going to die. It's already stopped eating."

"That's its own business!... Get away! You don't understand. If I told you, you still wouldn't understand."

Xiaoxiao sighed and looked at the old horse. With its eyes tightly closed, it rested its chin on the side of the trough, not looking, not eating. Under the pale yellow light, the horse's long thin face looked like a rock. If you stabbed it with a knife it probably wouldn't even flinch; it probably wouldn't even bleed. Mother said that people die, horses die, and then they all turn to rock.

Xiaoxiao went every day to see the old horse. He would watch it, bemused.

Tonight the moon was very bright. Its light seemed to penetrate the whole stable. The haystack cast a very long shadow, passing through the stable like a road, carrying the strange dreams of the world. Xiaoxiao was a little tired. He slid down from the top of the haystack. He wanted to walk along this road to the trough to get another handful of beans to chew, but then he suddenly heard footsteps. Someone flashed past and emerged from the back of the stable.

It was Mother. Xiaoxiao nearly called out to her. She had never come here before, and it was late...

Xiaoxiao drew back into the haystack to watch her. She walked to the front of the old horse, gathered together a mound of earth on the ground and stuck three sticks of incense into it. She lit them and, closing her eyes, put her palms together and mumbled a prayer to the tiny glowing red tips of the incense.

This was the first time Xiaoxiao had seen Mother come to burn incense for the horse. Curiously he walked to the front of the stable. He wanted to ask what she was doing. However, before he got near, Mother suddenly turned around, pulling a glistening object from her bosom —a dagger. It was the wooden-handled dagger with the dog carved on the handle, which Father kept in the glass cabinet.

"Mother!..." Xiaoxiao's voice quivered as though it would break.

"What are you doing here!" Mother's eyes were like two pieces of ice, so very cold. She hissed like a cat that has just seen a dog.

"What were you doing?"

"Go home to bed!" She pointed the dagger at him. The tip of that dagger concealed many inexplicable feelings. "I thought you were asleep..."

Xiaoxiao had no choice but to leave. As he went he saw his Mother's eyes fill with tears. Her tears would always collect in her eyes but never flow down her face. This made it harder for Xiaoxiao to bear.

Xiaoxiao couldn't sleep that night. His room was very spacious, but suddenly it became a black box, constricting him tightly until he was gasping for breath. Nor was it peaceful. In the middle of the night Father and Mother began to argue in the room where they ate dinner. Xiaoxiao quietly got up. He saw the dagger with a dog carved into its handle, cast aside on the floor. Although his parents weren't arguing very loudly, their faces were dark and heavy and their eyes were consumed with fire. One was looking at the floor and the other at the window.

"I tell you clearly, he won't be coming back. He died long ago on the Huma'er River."

This was Father's voice, hoarse as a pack of dogs running back from the grasslands with the wind.

"I'm begging you to kill that old horse soon. Don't let it suffer anymore." This was mother's voice. She spoke very quickly, without raising her head to look at Father.

"It's not painful. If you want to go to Huma'er River to look for him I can give you money and a horse. I'll give you whatever you need. But there is one condition. You must leave Xiaoxiao with me. He is my son."

"I don't want anything from you. Just kill that old horse soon. Don't let him suffer anymore."

Through all this, Mother was standing bolt upright in front of Father, her two hands grasping his arm. There were no tears in her eyes. This was the first time Xiaoxiao had seen his mother so brave and calm. She kicked the knife along the floor to Father's foot and said: "If you won't, then use that to kill me."

Father didn't dare meet Mother's eyes.

The two of them simply stood there in silence.

Suddenly, Mother bent down, picked up the dagger and thrust it into Father's hand. But, Father just raised his hand and threw the dagger out the open window. There was a vegetable patch outside, so it made no sound.

"You must live each and every day for me. The old horse must also live each and every day for me. Back then...it's a pity he fell off this horse into the Huma'er River. Otherwise...Hmph!"

Without even looking at Mother, Father turned and left. On the long, dark and narrow passage-way he kicked something that sounded like a frightened deer hitting itself up against the wooden wall.

The next morning, his parents behaved as though nothing had ever happened. As usual, they ate breakfast in the room, and as always the food was delicious. Father, holding a crumbling beef cake in his hands, let out a continuous wheezing and belching sound as he ate. Mother still sat on the stool silently drinking her sour milk, the snow-white nape of her neck exposed. Only Xiaoxiao didn't eat anything. To him, the soybean milk tasted raw.

From that day onwards that father began to speak even less. Sometimes Xiaoxiao wouldn't hear his voice for a whole day. He wouldn't even call out to the dogs when it was time to feed them. He wouldn't even move a muscle when the longhaired dog took off with the meat.

Many days passed. The wind was very cold, blowing until the stalks of the grass turned white and there were no leaves left on the trees. One day, the team of horses returned very late. A layer of glistening dew was draped over their backs so that they reflected the shining stars. Father's Dun River horse had been led back by a companion, but Father himself hadn't returned.

Obviously, something had happened! Xiaoxiao was worried about the old horse. He asked one of the workers, who just laughed and said nothing was wrong. But Xiaoxiao didn't believe that. He set out running towards the entrance of the village, followed by two dogs, running even faster than he was.

The dogs barked. Xiaoxiao could see the old horse on the grasslands road in the distance. Father and four workers had wrapped a leather rope around his stomach and were supporting him like a young bride as they slowly walked along. The old horse was completely covered in mud and so were Father and the four workers. They looked as if they had just fought a battle in the mud.

They took no notice of Xiaoxiao. Silently they walked past him, leaving a mess of muddy footprints on the road. What was wrong with the old horse? Didn't it want to go back to the stable? Xiaoxiao suddenly felt a kind of cold and detached grief. Even the two dogs hitting him with their wagging tails were like strangers to him.

Alone, he walked back to the yard. Mother was already waiting for him at the foot of the stairs of the *Mukeleng*.

"Where the hell did you run off to?" she demanded.

What did she mean by "where the hell?" He shot her a look of disapproval and, sticking out his chest, walked straight to the yard.

There the horse was being washed. Father was letting the workers stand and watch from the side. Slowly, he splashed water onto the back of the old horse with a wooden ladle and then brushed it down with the grass scrubbing brush. The sweat made channels in the mud on his naked back, like a shiny and transparent earthworm. He was very tall and although he was slightly stooped, he towered like a lofty haystack over the old horse.

Almost all the dogs in the yard had run over to them. Some sat, some stood, all quietly watching him brush the horse down. They were waiting for him to finish and feed them. When he finished brushing the horse he used a dry cloth to wipe its wet back, and then he tethered it to the trough. He seemed to have forgotten all about feeding those dogs. Without a glance at them he walked straight back to the *Mukeleng*.

"Xiaoxiao—! Xiaoxiao—! Where are you? Quickly, come home and eat dinner," Mother called to him in the usual way.

Xiaoxiao looked at the dogs with a feeling of utter helplessness, and ran to the two storey *Mukeleng*.

Every window was lit. This was Father's doing; even when he went to sleep he wouldn't let the lights be put out. They shone until bright day light. As well, in the middle of the night the swine would fire shots into the sky. The terrifying sound of gun shots would reverberate all night through the grasslands.

The staircase at the *Mukeleng* was very high. Layers of steam from the kitchen filled the air, layers of light blue, greyish white and pale yellow. Xiaoxiao pulled open the heavy oak door and bumped straight into Father.

"Where are you going? I haven't seen you since I came back!" He always talked as fiercely as this.

"I saw you. I was watching you the whole time you were brushing the horse."

The swine stood there woodenly. It was hard to tell if he was listening or not. His face tightened as hard as iron. It seemed as if he had something on his mind. He put his hand to his neck and continuously rubbed a dark purple scar, one he had received once from a knife wound.

His face was still set like iron during dinner. He didn't eat even one of the mutton rolls. He just drank one glass of wine after another until his eyes were bloodshot. Mother watched him silently. She seemed to know there was something worrying him.

After they had eaten, Mother cleared the table and went to the kitchen. Xiaoxiao was also about to leave when Father called him back: "Come over here!"

He scared Xiaoxiao with his bulging red eyes: "Take this jug of wine to the stable."

Then he called two shift workers over and told them to take all the dogs from the yard and lock them up: "Listen, no one is allowed to fire any shots tonight. If anyone fires a shot I will kill a horse and stuff him into the old horse's stomach."

The two men retreated gingerly. Xiaoxiao stood there watching as that swine walked impatiently up and down the floor, like a wild animal which had fallen into a pit trap.

Suddenly, he met Xiaoxiao's gaze and bellowed like a bull, "What are you still here for?"

Xiaoxiao walked to the front of the stable, took the two-handled jar of wine and placed it beside the haystack. He then took a handful of fried beans and placed them one by one into his mouth. He walked up to the old horse's head. It still looked as old as before, not eating and not moving. Its eyes, devoid of any brightness, were open wide as if it were waiting for something. It would be really awful if it were waiting for death. In his heart, Xiaoxiao knew he wouldn't just wait for that day. He would prepare himself a knife or a bullet.

That swine came in, carrying a lantern. Without looking at Xiaoxiao, he walked straight past him to the old horse. He took the lantern and placed it carefully on a rafter. He stroked the old horse's mane with one hand and placed the other under the horse's mouth. It was as if he was letting the old horse smell something on his hand, but there was nothing there.

"Where is my wine?" he asked suddenly, without even turning his head.

"Over there." Xiaoxiao quickly ran over and brought back the jug of wine.

Father removed the cork and slurped down a few mouthfuls. Then he poured some wine into the palm of his left hand and put it into the horse's mouth. After a long time, the old horse made two faint wheezing sounds. "You bastard, you're still alive," Father swore at the horse and laughed out aloud.

Father's hot breath smelt of wine, tobacco and something a lot like horse manure. His whole body reeked of horse manure.

"Why are you still here? Go home to bed!" he told Xiaoxiao, his gaze, cold and distant sending an icy current flowing into Xiaoxiao's body. Under the force of his stare, Xiaoxiao left, but he didn't go far. He circled around to the back of the stable and climbed into the haystack where he hid himself, showing only a pair of eyes.

That swine stripped off all his upper garments, baring his back. He picked up the straw cutter and under the lantern light he cut away at the straw, slice by slice. After a while, sweat started to pour from his back, like beads of oil. He cut the straw very finely—the same way that Mother sliced chives to make stuffing for the dumplings. He was well practised at this. He used the toe of one foot to hold the straw under the cutter as he sliced away at it, layer by layer. He might have cut straw for a lifetime. Even with his eyes closed he could cut it evenly.

He stopped cutting the straw and carefully picked out the leaves and twigs. He took some fried beans, crushed them in the roller and used water to mix it all thoroughly. Then with his hands he scooped the mixture into the trough.

The old horse hadn't eaten, and there was still no light in his staring eyes. Father stood by the trough watching silently and wiping the tobacco from his lips.

It was hard to know how long he stood there, face to face with the old horse. Xiaoxiao watched and watched from the top of the haystack, but nothing happened. Sleep oozed from his eyelids, gradually sticking them together. Then Mother called him again. He slid down the haystack and went back to his room to sleep.

The next day, the dawn came earlier than usual.

Xiaoxiao opened his eyes, slipped out from his quilt and ran to the stable. He didn't know whether anything had happened during the night; whether the dogs had barked or any shots had been fired.

Everything in front of the stable looked the same as last night. The two-handled wine jug was empty and the straw cutter had been thrown on the trough, along with father's clothes. The lantern on the rafter was still lit. But the old horse wasn't there.

With a feeling of complete loss, Xiaoxiao looked at the empty corner of the stable. He felt as if something heavy had hit him from behind. Where had the old horse gone? Remembering the cold and distant expression in father's eyes, he quickly ran to the *Mukeleng*.

He ran into the back room. It was empty except for a pot of hot milk on the table. Clearly, the swine hadn't eaten breakfast. He turned around and violently pushed open the kitchen door: "Where did Father go?"

"What's wrong? Xiaoxiao! Why did you fight with Father again?"

"No, I didn't...tell me, where has he gone?"

"I heard one of the workers say that he has left the village. What has happened?"

"The old horse is missing."

"The old horse..."

Tears suddenly flowed from Mother's eyes.

Xiaoxiao didn't stop to ask why Mother was crying. Without pausing even for a second he flew out of the *Mukeleng*. In the yard the sound of his footsteps frightened the chickens and with an explosion they flew off in all directions. The dogs also fled into the distance.

He ran out of the village. He ran all the way to the mouth of the road that passed through to the end of the grasslands.

That swine was standing there, his back bared and his neck bent. To the front of him stood the forest of willows, now nearly bare of all their leaves. Behind him lay the main road.

A low fine spray of pale blue mist was slowly spreading across the early morning grasslands. It had spread underneath that swine's feet. It seemed he had been there for a very, very long time. He was like a large rock that had been placed there.

"Father—! Father—!"

Xiaoxiao called loudly to him as he ran over but the swine didn't move at all. He didn't seem to have heard that heart-rending call.

"Father—! Father—!"

The swine of a man still didn't move. His long hair blew about in the wind like a disorderly clump of grass.

"Father, the old horse?"

Father didn't answer. His face was expressionless. Xiaoxiao could clearly see two tracks of tears on either side of his face. Even *he* could cry?

Only then Xiaoxiao saw the new grave beneath his father's feet. Footprints were trampled into the black earth and evenly sized stones were arranged in a circle around it. There was a pickaxe and an old split-bladed spade lying beside it.

"Is that the old horse's grave? Is he dead?..."

The swine glanced angrily at Xiaoxiao. He squatted on the ground and buried his face deep in his hands.

How could the old horse have died?

Xiaoxiao felt that the grasslands were filled with the smell of wine, tobacco and horse manure.

Old Stick's Wine Shop

Translated by T. Nelson

That old bastard, he always used raw charcoal to warm up the wine, just to save money. Dense suffocating smoke hung in the room, wandering back and forth along the table tops like a herd of sheep. After one whiff of this raw smoke, Three Kick Chen's desire for the wine abated considerably.

He could smell the odor even before he turned his sleigh into the wine shop yard. He had a sharp sense of smell. When he was younger and lived up in the mountains, he had been able to judge when a wild beast had passed through, just by smelling the manure heap.

More than ten horses were tethered in the yard, which was crowded with people. "One Eye" from the Yuansheng Store was there bartering with some Oroqen traders who were exchanging skins, roots and herbs, for salt, gunpowder and flour. Everyone knew perfectly well that by dealing with "One Eye" they would be cheated, but they weren't willing to travel another one hundred and fifty *li* to do business at the Lower Village Government Store. A heavy snow storm that would seal the mountain pass was coming from the west. Before the mountain pass was closed they needed to find a place to stay, and there was still a lot to do.

There were people everywhere. The snow on the ground had been trampled into mud. A thin layer of ice had formed on the top, shining black and oily. "One Eye" held an ebony abacus in one hand, using the other to wipe the sticky gum out of his dead eye with the sleeve of his jacket. His dead eye was the result of being stabbed by a local hunter during a fight over a woman. If it hadn't been for that, he would have gone to Egunei River and probably made his fortune within three or five years. As it was, he couldn't read characters, let alone use an abacus. However, his tongue was quicker than any abacus and he could talk those Oroqen traders into a daze. Three Kick Chen didn't need to listen very hard; with one glance he could pick up all the subtleties of what was happening around him. He could sense that "One Eye" was very interested in some marten furs. However, he wasn't willing to say anything and ruin the "sale." It wasn't worth it to him to interfere with other people's business. He needed to save all his energy for himself.

As his sleigh entered the enclosure, people leapt aside like frightened deer, and they glared at him angrily.

He knew why these people were scared. They thought he was an apparition. "He is still alive. How is it possible that Three Kick Chen isn't dead?" He wasn't mistaken! That was definitely what they were thinking.

They watched him as he heaved the short-faced bear from the sleigh. The bear weighed at least four hundred pounds, and left a deep impression in the mud. A knife had entered its pharynx and ripped down, splitting it completely open, spilling its intestines from its body and smashing its balls.

"Hey, Master Foot, what do you have to trade?" "One Eye" called, laughing until his face was burning.

Three Kick Chen didn't glance at him, but squatted down and untied the horse's belt.

"Within three days the mountain pass will be sealed, Master Foot. You can pick something from here in exchange for your draught animal," he said.

Three Kick Chen tethered his horse to the stake and walked over to the bear saying, "Trade it my foot, you bastard! Get me two men to carry it inside."

Opening his eyes widely, he swept his glance over the people in the yard, as if they were a bunch of idiots. When he was in the forest he never saw any sign of them, even though they too depended on the forest for their livelihood. He still had sharp eyes that cut like a knife. Around these parts he was a man with a big reputation, not that he paid it any heed. There wasn't a man or dog here who didn't know him. They were all scared of him, including the women. He was extremely brave and wielded a knife with great skill. He broke his toe once, killing a wolf with three kicks. Everyone called him "Yellow Haired Chen" behind his back. However, none of them could guess how old he was, whether he had been married, which woman he had loved or whether he was a Han Chinese or a Tahur. He had never been known to smile. Nothing he ever did seemed to make him happy, not even drinking wine.

Three Kick Chen went into the wine shop and sat at the table next to the window, which he opened, allowing the wind to flow in and the smoke to drift out.

Old Stick stood by the fire slicing radish on a cutting board. Whenever he came, Three Kick Chen would always eat a large bowl of sugared radish sticks.

"It must be three or four months since you've been here." With eyes like the wicks of an oil lamp Old Stick looked Three Kick Chen up and down.

"I nearly didn't get to see you." Three Kick Chen ripped the beef in the bowl into shreds.

"Are you talking about the incident at Xinzi Gully?"

"That's right. I walked that road for over a month."

"You walked? I heard that they had heavy snow there last month."

"On the day the heavy snows came I was on a boat at the mouth of the Huma'er River. At Raozhu we encountered strong winds. The waves on the Heilong River were higher than the mast, tossing the boat up and crashing it against the shore. Afterwards, we couldn't salvage even one whole wooden plank."

"What happened to the people on the boat?" Old Stick asked.

"Well, I was one of them! The owner of the boat died. His whole family died, his wife and children—the youngest was only one week old. He disappeared completely—they couldn't even find his body. But I haven't forgotten that he still owes me twenty gold pieces."

"That debt will have to be paid now in the other world," remarked Old Stick.

"I never intended to make him pay back the money. I just wanted him to remember. After all, even his boat was bought with the money I gave him. I did that because he seemed like a real man, and he was a newcomer here..."

The sugared radish sticks were served. As Three Kick Chen munched like a cow chewing its cud, washing it down with his wine, his Adam's apple, covered in a red rash, rumbled as it moved. Then he swore, complaining that the wine was diluted with water and that the radish sticks weren't sweet or crisp enough.

Old Stick stood silently to the side, bowing ingratiatingly as he listened. However, his eyes flickered like oil-lamp wicks, letting out a dim blue light as he ground his teeth together tightly. He hated this Yellow Beard. From the first day he had opened his business here ten years ago, Three Kick Chen had come and gone—eating and drinking but never paying.

Although Three Kick Chen hadn't lifted his head, he could guess what was going through Old Stick's mind as he watched the latter drinking his wine. In his eyes, Old Stick was merely an injured wolf. Chen was very pleased with the name "Old Stick." After all, it was he who first gave him the name Old Stick. When this Green Bean Eyes had first arrived from south of the wall, still unsure of his surroundings, they had had a trial of strength. This occurred the second time they met—on the road. Three Kick Chen stood his horse across the road and turned a curved knife more than a foot long over in his hand. His eyes were fixed on Green Bean Eyes as if he were admiring a hunted animal. "You must have made a fortune to be coming here." Green Bean Eyes was momentarily seized with terror. Quickly he calmed himself and replied, "That's none of your business." Three Kick Chen said, "You obviously haven't been here long. Everyone knows that this knife of mine loves to concern itself with other people's business."

Green Bean Eyes stared fixedly at the knife flying up and down in his opponent's hand, and at the yellow beard that looked like matted grass. "I'm a trader. I've come here to run a business."

Three Kick Chen said, "You can't hide the truth from my eyes. I spend the whole day around wild beasts. My nose is good. I can tell that you've killed at least two people. Your body still smells fishy."

Green Bean Eyes was both flustered and anxious. "You really shouldn't make unfounded and malicious attacks on people. This is no joking matter." Before his voice had even reached the ground, his rabbit skin hat had been jabbed from his head. Three Kick Chen then pressed the knife up against his throat and said, "You bastard! You old stick! If you still consider yourself a man, then you had better behave yourself around here. If you cause me any trouble, I will send you away from here—your head in one direction and your body in the other."

Since then, Three Kick Chen had not brought this incident up again; however what he had said still weighed like a rock on Old Stick's mind.

Old Stick wanted him to clear his debt—he remembered exactly how much was owed him. Friendship was friendship and business was business.

And what friendship did he have with this "Yellow Hair" anyway? Simply thinking of the hard ringworm scabs on the latter's body made him itch. In the last few months there had been no news whatsoever of Three Kick Chen. He would say to anyone who was passing through, "Three Kick Chen, that old bugger, still owes me a sum of wine money. He doesn't even leave a fart. How can he call himself a man!"—These words came back to him now, sticking like a bullet in his throat. But he didn't say them out aloud.

Three Kick Chen slammed the two-handled copper wine jar in front of him.

"Give me another jar."

"You want more to drink?"

"Are you worried I'm not going to pay you your wine money?"

"It's not worth my worrying about this small amount of money," said Old Stick.

"I won't cheat you of your money. I'm the kind of person who lives with a clear conscience and dies honestly."

Old Stick laughed drily as he filled the jar with wine. He sat down on a stool opposite Three Kick Chen. Just at that instant he noticed the towel inside Chen's half-opened jacket, soaked black with blood. There was a large wound from his neck cutting deep down into his body. As he breathed in and out, blood oozed from the recently congealed scar. Old Stick was a little surprised, but also somewhat pleased. It didn't matter who had done this. It had been done well. This is retribution, he thought.

To him, Three Kick Chen's face looked like a burnt tattered cloth. He had sprinkled it with sorghum wine, but it still looked as though life was about to be extinguished. No wonder he pulled his hat down so low, Old Stick thought. He wasn't willing to let anyone see his wound or his face. He wanted the people who knew him to remember him as the proud and honorable person he had been.

He didn't have much time left. Old Stick suddenly felt that he should forget the debt and stop hating him. But he didn't know what to say. Should he try to comfort him or should he swear at him?

"Damn it, you! What are you staring at inside my jacket?"

"What? Nothing. I can't see anything."

Even though Three Kick Chen didn't look at him, but continued to sit there with his eyes closed, sipping constantly at his wine, Old Stick still felt a cold draft pass over his body, chilling him to the bone. His voice began to tremble. He knew that Three Kick Chen wasn't willing to let him see his wound. What's more, he knew this devil would do anything in order to ensure his silence.

"This time someone's wish has been granted, but I won't give him the pleasure of gossiping about it," Chen said.

"You're not badly wounded are you?"

"I still have breath left in me," Three Kick Chen took the hunting knife from his waist, placed it on the table and said, "Go and get your account book and bring it here."

"No, Master Foot, that wasn't what I meant," Old Stick protested.

"I want you to write down who owes me money." Three Kick Chen watched as Old Stick brought out the account book and his inkstone, then Chen reached inside his shirt and scratched the itchy parts of his wound. Closing his eyes he slowly started to speak, "Scar Eye Zhang owes me twenty gold pieces; Zhang Zhao, the bastard, owes me one bushel of wheat and four gold pieces; Lu Laoliu owes me money for two bear paws and ten gold pieces; Whiskers Liu owes me six horses..."

Old Stick wrote it all down stroke by stroke. Then he asked, "Is that the lot?"

Three Kick Chen drank a mouthful of wine and said, "That's all there is."

"Were you thinking of using these for your wine money?" Old Stick asked.

"I just want to make sure they remember that they all owe me money. In the future maybe they won't do so many awful things. Wang Fengxiong died. He brought three of them and there was only one of me to fight them. They did a terrible thing to Widow Zhang. They deserved all they got. He met up with me at the mouth of the Naren River, and died on the end of my knife."

"Yes, he deserved what he got."

"They left this bear behind. That fellow, Wang Fengxiong, was an exceptional shot with a gun. It's a real shame he met up with me, but he has only got himself to blame for committing so many atrocities."

He snorted. Probably because it hurt, his face became extremely pale.

"Take this bear to the Lower Valley Government Store and trade it for some flour. There is also this purse of money. I want you to give it all to Widow Zhang." He pulled a dogskin purse from his waist and threw it with a bang onto the table.

Old Stick took the dogskin purse, weighed it in his hand and said, "I heard that when you were young, you and Widow Zhang had something going..."

Three Kick Chen stood up, towering over Old Stick. He grabbed his collar and using all his strength he twisted it until Old Stick's face changed to the color of grey earth and his two green bean eyes bulged out. He held up his fist and shook it in front of Old Stick's nose.

"If your bones are itching I can use these two hands to fix them,' Three Kick Chen warned.

He loosened his hold and Old Stick fell to the floor.

The wine shop was as quiet as death. The few people who had been drinking inside had all left. The people in the courtyard had also dispersed.

Three Kick Chen sat down again. He poured all the wine from the jar into his bowl. "Look at me," he said, "all my life I have eaten, drunk, been around and been merry, and I've never owed anybody anything. Make sure you remember today's wine money. When the time comes, someone will repay you. If you remember this you haven't lived in vain."

"You don't have any sons or daughters. What are you going to repay me with?" demanded Old Stick.

"I have forty-two scars on my body. You've seen them. Now a new one has been added. They are like gold."

"That they are. How could I not understand this? I'm not going to press you."

"Whether you press me or not, I'll settle with you."

"No, no, that's not what I meant!" Old Stick felt a cold draft of fear rise from under his feet. He began to shake until his teeth were chattering.

Three Kick Chen removed the gold ring from his finger.—It was a ring that he had made in Harbin. On it was engraved the figure of a dog. It was said that this dog had been with him for half of his life. Someone had stolen it, beaten it to death, eaten its flesh and then actually sent the dogskin for him to see. At that time he had been overcome with grief and anger, stabbing himself in the throat. Fortunately, he had been found before it was too late. Otherwise he would have drunk far fewer barrels of wine! —He placed the ring in Old Stick's hand and said, "Remember this clearly. Go to Moleng and find Liu Santai. Give this ring to him and ask him for the wine money. He will repay you every penny."

Old Stick weighed the ring in his hand. From handling the ring, a sudden realisation dawned on him and he sat there in a daze for a long time. "You are just going to leave like that? And not come back to my wine shop and drink my wine?"

"That's right. I'm going and I won't be back."

"You're not coming back?"

"I'm not coming back."

"Where are you going?"

"I'm going to Xiaosu Gully in Moleng Mountain. I came from that gold mine. I want to go back there."

"You must be crazy! You've got wounds on your body...the mountain will be sealed with snow within three days...if you're not careful you will freeze to death on the road..."

"Oh, you think I'll freeze to death, do you?" Three Kick Chen snorted with amusement. He drank mouthful after mouthful of the wine from the copper jar. He hung his hunting knife back from his waist and draped the large leopard skin around his shoulders. Then he put on his fox skin hat and, like a big black bear, he pushed open the door and walked away.

Old Stick followed him into the courtyard and blocked Three Kick Chen's path before he could lead his horse away. "I still say you should stay here for a couple of days and let your wounds heal before you leave," he said.

Three Kick Chen stared ferociously at Old Stick. "Let my wounds heal? What, do you want all the people here to know that I am lying in your house wounded!?" He harnessed his horse, got on his sleigh and left.

The night fell in the north-western sky. Clouds pressed down on the mountains and the forests loomed like a group of black wild beasts, lying in wait for his sleigh.

All this happened last year. That was also the last time Old Stick saw Three Kick Chen. It seemed also that when he left he had taken something from Old Stick's heart with him. All winter Old Stick had languished, his heart empty. Winter was a time when the wine shop brought in the most money, because you could dilute the wine with large amounts of water. But because he hadn't received any news about Three Kick Chen, Old Stick was like a rabbit hidden in a hole. He had lost weight and all day long he would drink from the copper jar until he was dizzy. He felt that he was as useless as his immobile wine shop.

He didn't understand. Why had Three Kick Chen "gone" like that? What a life he had had—people had called him a hard man, a hero, some even said he was a "devil," or a "barbarian." But after he left there wasn't a man who didn't think about him. Many young people even dyed their beards yellow, and wore large leopard skin coats and three-cornered fox skin caps to be like him. Even "One Eye" made a special trip over to give Old Stick ten *jin* of top grade tobacco from the northeast to take to Three Kick Chen. He said he had also stayed at Xiaosu Gully gold mine.

The snow finally melted and spring arrived. But who was the grass turning green for?

People went in groups from the town to Xiaosu Gully to try to learn if there was any news of Three Kick Chen. But there was none. It was as if he had never been here, or as if he had flowed away with the snow as it melted in the spring breeze.

Old Stick also went to Xiaosu Gully, carrying the ten pounds of tobacco as well as a barrel of wine and many pounds of beef. On the way back he made a detour through Moleng to look for Liu Santai.

The village was about the same size as the palm of his hand. He didn't know Liu Santai, but he knew if he stood on the street and shouted his name, Liu Santai would come.

But he hadn't dreamed that the Liu Santai who would come and stand in front of him would be a thirteen or fourteen year old child, wearing a hollow cotton padded jacket hanging open, with a face, hands and chest as red as a radish. This child aroused Old Stick's curiosity.

"Are you really called Liu Santai?"

The child very calmly replied, "This town doesn't have another Liu Santai. What do you want with me? Why have you come looking for me?"

"Do you know Three Kick Chen?"

"I know him," the child said.

"He asked me to give you this ring."

"Is he dead?"

"I don't know. Last year, before the mountain was sealed with snow, he went to Xiaosu Gully."

"He won't be coming back, then."

"How do you know?" asked Old Stick.

"When I was ten, he told me that when he was ready to die, he would go to Xiaosu Gully and not return. He didn't want everyone to see him die. Did he say anything to you before he left?"

"Only this, that you would pay his wine money."

"Wine money? All right, I will pay you," Liu Santai said.

"You're not even as tall as a rifle. What are you going to pay me with?"

"Don't worry. As soon as I am grown up I will repay every penny. You must be Old Stick!"

In a challenging way he slapped the ring into Old Stick's hand. "You must stick around and wait for me. For the time being, use this as a guarantee. When I give you the wine money you must return the ring to me. If you lose it, I won't forgive you."

Without waiting for Old Stick to ponder about this, Liu Santai left.

Old Stick stood there. The more he thought about what the boy had said, the warmer he felt, since he could believe everything was in order. He shouted after the child, "You don't have to pay back Old Stick's money!"

He didn't know whether the child heard or not. The boy didn't look back, but kept walking into the distance. Old Stick could see clearly that the leather belt he was wearing was Three Kick Chen's.

Still he stood there, staring blankly down at the dog on the face of the ring, his old eyes full of tears. Under the pale and distant sunlight, both the ring and the old man's tears glistened.

The Gorge
Translated by R. O'Hanlan-Mullar

The three horses worked their way through the forest; after walking for a full four hours, they stopped.

"We'll tie up the horses here." Shenken jumped down, without even glancing at Bieerdan and Enduli by his side.

There was a withered tree that had been dead for many years. Next to this tree was a camphor pine as thick as a bear's waist. The wet sap, following the rough contours of the bark, flowed straight down into a crack in the rock at the base of the tree. At eye level, a piece of bark had been peeled away from the tree trunk. Above it an image of the face of 'Bainaqia' (the mountain god) had been carved with a knife. The pointy nose had been rubbed so often that it had become shiny. But its two concave eyes had a mysterious, frightening feeling about them.

"The cave is still a long way from here," Bieerdan muttered.

"Have you damn well killed a bear before?!!" Shenken did not even turn his head. He was facing the high and steep Lele Mountain, covered with multicoloured birch trees. The village was still warm and families had not yet cut the *rutabaga*, but here the first snow of winter had already fallen. The snow was very light, but the snowflakes were as hard as sand. The low-lying places were all white. However, the higher places were bare, a metallic grey colour all over. There was a ferocious wind atop the mountain peak. A person would not be able to stand up, and the trees were all bent over towards the darkened gorge.

Enduli used the back of his knife to knock a nail into his saddle. His backside suffered immensely because of the oak-wood pack saddle. While he knocked he looked askance at Shenken's back. His knocking made a loud sound, and the whole mountain was filled with it.

Bieerdan understood clearly why he was knocking in such a way. The nail was rusted, so it would not make any difference if he knocked it or not. Standing quite far away, Bieerdan also stared fixedly at Shenken's back as he swung a hunting knife back and forth, stabbing repeatedly at a camphor pine. He really admired the way Enduli was knocking. He also hoped that the sound would irritate Shenken, and that they would quarrel again, and maybe even use the knife. He and Enduli had discovered the bear, and they did not want to have this adult come and butt in, an adult who said the bear was "his."

They were not children anymore; hunting required real men. Here, children became adults very early. Although they were only fourteen or fifteen years old, and they had only just learnt to ride horses and shoot a gun, they had already clashed with the adults.

Bieerdan had run away before, and been brought back to be flogged with a whip by his father. But he had not shed one tear. He did not understand why his brother was allowed to go hunting in the mountain, but he was not. His brother was only three years older than he, and was not as tall.

His mother had taken sides with his brother: "Your brother killed a bear by himself." What was that bear worth anyway? A bear cub, which was not even two hundred pounds, the skin of which was still hung up back there at home, and not much bigger than a roe deer.

He wanted to shoot a big one, at least four hundred pounds. The bear he and Enduli had seen at the bottom of Lele Mountain the day before yesterday was a full five or six hundred pounds. It was walking along heavily, swaying from side to side as if half its body was paralyzed. Many times the bear had wanted to stand up to pull down the pine cones from the trees, but it failed each time. They could only watch as it pushed its way back into its cave, which was covered by a thicket of mountain birch and climbing pine. They had not brought a gun. Nor did they did own their own gun. They had to do whatever the adults said. Sooner or later, they both thought, we will have to become adults, but neither said it aloud.

The next day, the day after they had discovered the bear cave, they had stealthily returned to the village. They did not dare return home. If they had, the adults would have caught them like chickens, and locked them into the *xierenzhu*, and they would not have been let out for days. Never mind bears, even if it were a dragon they would not be able to set eyes on it. In any case, the adults would not listen to what they said. So they simply went to their relatives and borrowed guns and horses, telling them a false story. Adults are exceptionally foolish sometimes; they are so very self-satisfied.

It was on the road into the mountain that the boys ran into the old guy Shenken. Shenken had left the village before they were born. They had heard that he had offended "Toulunmalu," the witchdoctor. When Toulunmalu was performing, Shenken had started laughing, and everybody chased him out of the village. Shenken said that when the witchdoctor was dancing his trousers had nearly fallen down, and he had seen the witchdoctor's exposed backside! Shenken was certainly not much good: why would he want to look at someone's backside? Also, Shenken had stolen watermelons from Wurina's place. He said, "The watermelons from that girl's place are delicious. If they weren't from the girl's place I wouldn't have stolen them!"

Up until now Shenken had not managed to get himself a wife. He was exceptionally clever with his knife though, and could, with both eyes closed, throw the knife accurately for a long way.

"Oh, it's you two!" He was playing with his knife as he spoke. He nailed a grey ratskin full of holes onto a tree trunk.

His eyes were glowing red; he had evidently drunk too much wine. "You'd better get out of my way."

"But we just want to go to Lele Mountain." Bieerdan courteously jumped down from his horse.

"That won't be possible. I am waiting for a stag deer right now. I've been waiting for it for three days already," said Shenken.

"The bear cave that we want to block up is on Lele Mountain." Bieerdan's voice rose.

"Just the two of you sticks of firewood going to hunt a bear? Heh, heh, heh," he laughed strangely. "I'm telling you again that the bear is mine. I want it to feed for a few more days and wait until the snow is a bit thicker, and then go and hunt it."

"You're still saying that the bear is yours?" Still on his horse, Enduli pushed one bullet into the bore of the gun with a click.

"Ha! So you can shoot, too, child? Try this then...!" He untied his deer skin clothes, to reveal a chestful of measle spots.

Enduli was startled, lowering the barrel of the gun and saying, "We're the ones who found the bear cave!"

"That damned bear has been on Lele Mountain for many decades, heh, heh, heh. How many days have you two been out of your mothers' wombs?" Shenken laughed strangely again, and walked to the front of his horse, straightening up his saddle pack and saying, "You will never defeat that old bear! Without me, you won't beat that old bear!"

Bieerdan and Enduli blocked Shenken's horse. "We don't need you!" they retorted.

"Without me, you're just throwing your bones onto the mountain!" Shenken raised his reins and charged between their horses, separating them. "That old bear is the spirit of Lele Mountain!"

He went on his way, and the two borrowed horses seemed to recognise him as a leader and followed closely behind.

"What point is there in bringing a gun to hunt a bear? You can't use a gun to hunt a bear." He sat assuredly on his saddle, with one hand reaching in to scratch his breast, whilst he put dried roe deer meat and tobacco tips together into his mouth with the other. "A bear cannot be killed recklessly. It will come to you when it's time for it to die. You both know that we Oroqens and the bears are of the one family. I call the old bear on Lele Mountain 'Amaha' (Uncle). What are you laughing at? You two fools! That bear is really and truly my 'Amaha'."

"He's drunk," Bieerdan said to Enduli. He kept his voice low, but Shenken still overheard him.

"I'm drunk? Could I get drunk on one bag of wine?" He roared loudly, and his two timeworn eyes gave a red glow. "How many people who hunt these days know that originally bears were also human, and that they are the result of the transformation of a girl wearing a red bracelet? None of them are good hunters."

He went on to talk about how to use a knife when hunting bears. It seemed that it was all based on other people's experience, because Bieerdan and Enduli had never heard of Shenken's hunting down a bear before. Once, when he had contracted some eye disease, he had to go to the Naji house to borrow a bear gall to put on his eyes.

The other two pulled away a little distance from Shenken, as they had no desire to listen to his telling tall stories while he was drinking. They actually despised even more the adult in front of them.

It would be great if there were another road going into Lele Mountain, both of them wished unhappily.

They knew that they must either separate, or fight it out properly... Bieerdan looked meaningfully at Enduli, but Enduli was still knocking the rusted nail on his horse saddle.

Shenken was riding his horse, drinking a bit of wine. He took a bunch of tobacco tips from his roe deer leather bag, and a few stiff pieces of dried roe deer meat, and stuffed them into his mouth together, chewing gurglingly, loudly, like a pig.

"Have we dawdled long enough? Let's go!" Shenken's throat was bobbing up and down like a chicken's bottom, swallowing the tobacco tips and dried roe deer meat with a rumble. He tightened his deerskin overcoat and walked towards Enduli.

"We two won't be going with you." Bieerdan's hand gripped the *Bieladanka* rifle tightly.

"That's right." Enduli's hand holding the gun trembled slightly. He did not dare look at Shenken's reddening eyes. He was the one who had made Bieerdan come and hunt the bear. On a *Muluobei* (birch bark boat), Enduli could cast a hook and spear fish very gracefully. He could also carve all kinds of birch cases. There was no point in his ascending the mountain to hunt the bear; he had already proved himself an adult, an exceptionally competent and brave fellow. Many girls in the village were pursuing him and all of them were older than he.

"I've said it before, you can't take a gun to hunt a bear." Shenken heard the sound of the gun's primer bolt being pulled back behind him. His squat face became serious, as though he had smeared a thick layer of bear oil all over it. "If you use a gun in hunting, there will be no bears on Lele Mountain again. The trees up there will all dry up and die and the grass will not grow. We need the mountain to provide us with life."

The stench of raw tobacco came from his mouth. Bieerdan attempted to seize the gun, but without success because the other was too powerful. Bieerdan did not understand how that pair of shrivelled hands could have so much power. It seemed almost as if the gun had grown in his hand.

"If you don't let go I'll shoot!" Bieerdan warned.

"Don't shoot, Bieerdan! Don't shoot! Maybe..." said Enduli, taking pity on Shenken all of a sudden. He saw that Shenken's elk leather trouser legs were already dreadfully tattered.

The holes had been sewn up with thick deer sinews, but Shenken's flesh was still exposed. The pair of elk skin boots were not even worth mentioning. They were simply tied onto his feet with deer sinews. It looked as if it would take at least an hour for him to remove his boots; or maybe it had been a long, long time since he had taken them off. The life of a man without a woman is hard.

"Let him come with us," Enduli asked Bieerdan placatingly. Even he himself could not say clearly why he had hated Shenken so much only a moment before.

"Yes. I just want to go and hunt the bear. I don't want anything to be divided up between us. I don't even want one piece of the meat." Shenken turned to face the ravine's uneven tree line, and the blue mist floating over the surface of the trees. "I just want you to give Wurina a message. Greet her and ask her to marry someone far away. I have no face, no dignity, left to return to the village, and I am too ashamed to see her."

His voice floated into the wind which hummed through the top of the grass that lay all around the spring.

Bieerdan and Enduli were frightened. They did not understand what Shenken had said. The girl Wurina had refused to marry anyone; she did not even dare to come out of her house. What did all this have to do with him?

As the three pushed through the undergrowth in the ravine, the distance between them increased. The grass was very thick in the ravine.

The fallen leaves were also very thick, and a deep layer of snow covered the ground. When their boots sank into the snow, they made a wet, squeaky sound.

Shenken's boots would certainly be soaked through, Enduli thought. Since he did not want even one piece of bear meat, why did he still want to go up the mountain with them?

Bieerdan deliberately shook the water from his socks so that it splashed onto Shenken's back. Shenken did not feel it. He was still chattering incessantly, telling the history of Lele Mountain and the affairs of those old fellows, drinking wine continuously and chewing his dried roe deer meat and tobacco tips.

He talked on and on, but Bieerdan and Enduli were not listening very intently. They did not know what use the history of Lele Mountain and the affairs of those old men were to them.

"You shouldn't hunt small deer, and you can't hunt a single deer either. If you want to hunt, you should kill male and female together. If you leave one alive, it will be very sad, just as a living person would be. Are you listening carefully? More important, you can't go after a deer that's been injured. Hunting an injured deer, how heroic is that? Turds! Bastards...!"

He suddenly broke off as he seemed to step down onto nothing, falling into a small waterhole. From a distance Bieerdan and Enduli watched him as he climbed out awkwardly to stand on a hilly mound of grass, stupefied.

"My tobacco bag has fallen into the water." He was talking to himself while staring fixedly at the surface of the water, which gurgled and bubbled.

"I had only this one bag of tobacco tips. Now that this has happened, I won't be able to taste tobacco for another two weeks. If it had been a bag of dried roe deer meat that fell in, I wouldn't have cared. I've had enough of eating that tasteless stuff."

But Lele Mountain was in front of them.

The fallen pine needles became more and more dense. The light snow, stuck to the rocks and the grass, was dry and hard, and very slippery. Since losing his tobacco bag, Shenken had not said one word. He was as dexterous as a deer, climbing very lightly and nimbly to the mountain peak. Who would have believed that he was already fifty years old?

The wind at the peak was so strong that a person could not lift his head. Enduli clambered up to the peak, and his whole being seemed to be seized by a strange sound. The sound seemed to penetrate right into his skull and senses, squeezing everything out of his body. It made his head swell suddenly, and his legs felt as though he had trodden on something as soft as cotton.

"Is that the bear growling?" His voice shook slightly.

"I haven't heard a bear growling before." Bieerdan had shivered too.

"That is not a bear growling." Shenken's clothes were wet and it was getting cool, so he was coughing incessantly. "It's the sound of the water in the gorge."

They went around the peak to the northern face, a slow gradual slope which was covered with mountain birch and climbing pine. Below this was the mouth of the cave, flat and dark like the mouth of a bear. The three of them caught sight of the cave mouth at the same time, and slowly edged over to it. They soon approached the expanse of climbing pine.

Shenken indicated to Bieerdan and Enduli that they should stop and hide behind a maple pine tree. He continued to walk ahead. He found a few tufts of bear fur on the climbing pine and concluded that this was a bear's cave. He also deduced that the bear had gone into the cave a few days previously and was still in there.

"Go and chop a few birch wood poles," Shenken ordered.

Bieerdan and Enduli both listened carefully to what he said. They were impressed because Shenken had seen those few tufts of bear fur. That confirmed Shenken's experience, and gave them confidence in him.

They used a few birch wood poles to block up the mouth of the cave haphazardly, in order to break the advance of the charging bear. In an instant the whole mountain seemed terrifying. And there was no one else to come and share this fear with them.

"You use those birch wood poles to poke at it," said Shenken.

"And you?"

Shenken headed backwards. He retreated further and further and stopped under a maple pine tree a full fifty meters from the mouth of the cave. He held the knife horizontally in his hand, and bent down saying, "When the bear comes out of the cave, it won't be able to turn around, so there's no danger for you. I'll wait here for it."

The knife in Shenken's hand was very bright and the expression in his eyes also seemed as sharp as the knife. The boys' hearts seemed to be affected by the radiance, and their fear dissipated. A wave of fervor reached to their every fingertip.

Hunting is ultimately something for young people. And these boys' eyes were all alight with their enthusiasm.

"Grrr..."

A sinister roar came out of the cave. It pealed out like a clap of thunder and seemed to shake the whole of Lele Mountain. It seemed as though the grass, the climbing pine branches and the small trees near the mouth of the cave had all been simultaneously blown over by a wind, flattened by the tearing low howl.

Bieerdan and Enduli used their birchwood poles to poke downwards, but without the slightest result. Cautiously they leaned forward a little more. This enabled them to see the receding road much more clearly. They poked with their birchwood poles a little more deeply, not yet having used up all their strength. The roaring continued. It seemed as though it was right in their ears, shattering their eardrums. It was the first time they had heard a bear roaring. The deep sound scared them senseless and they fell onto the climbing pine.

When they had recovered a little, they stood up on the climbing pine, and suddenly discovered that Shenken was not behind the maple pine tree. There was no shadow or trace of him. Where had the fellow gone? And his shining knife?

Bieerdan and Enduli exchanged astonished glances. Their thoughts had hardly registered, though, when a dark object rushed out from the cave, heading straight past them. Both of their bodies were hit by the birchwood poles that had blocked up the mouth of the cave and they fell heavily to the ground.

Bieerdan's face was cut. Enduli lost the knife out of his hand and his right shoulder was wounded so badly that his whole arm was immobilised.

"Let's run, quickly! Hurry and get the gun." Bieerdan's voice changed pitch.

Neither of them knew where the burst of strength had come from. They swiftly left the peak, descending the mountain without taking a breath. Their clothes were torn by the edges of rocks and tree branches. The wind bore in through the holes in their clothes and made every joint go cold.

Bieerdan was running and cursing. "Whoever heard of a hunter who doesn't bring a gun? It's all that bastard Shenken's fault."

When he and Enduli had almost arrived at the place where the horses were tied up, they both stopped nervously. They saw Shenken sitting securely on his horse, looking as if a layer of frost had been smeared on his face.

"I really couldn't stand it." Shenken's body slumped forwards, his head drooped down, and he covered his eyes with his hands. "I couldn't stand the bear's howling. It's not a male bear, it's a pregnant bear and about to give birth. Couldn't you hear it? It howled as if it were weeping..."

Enduli pulled Shenken from his horse. "Don't talk rubbish!" he cried angrily. "You ran away so fast and didn't let us take a gun. You wanted to destroy us deliberately."

"Beat him up! He's not a man!" Bieerdan charged towards Shenken.

They beat him to the ground. His mouth started to bleed. He stood up slowly, using his hand to wipe the blood from near his mouth into it, swallowing it and saying, "It was crying, I swear, it was crying..."

"You just left us up there and ran!" Enduli gasped out hoarsely. It had been his fist on Shenken's face. It was the first time Enduli had hit a man and he had not expected him to bleed. Enduli was choked with nervousness.

"I really couldn't stand it," was all that Shenken could say.

"Don't pay any attention to him. Let's go!" Bieerdan picked up the gun, loaded the bullets and headed up the mountain without turning back.

Enduli followed closely, walking and loading his gun. His pace was very brisk. It was the first time he had felt courage, the courage of a real man.

Shenken was staring as the boys walked further away. He suddenly thought of something, and he called out in a loud voice, "Don't use the gun to hurt her! Enduli! Bieerdan! You can't use a gun to hurt her! Let her give birth to the cub—it's going to be born soon."

He sounded as though he was crying and his voice seemed to shake the whole gorge. Bieerdan and Enduli did not hesitate for a second. It felt as though a gust of wind had blown out from beneath their feet. The mountain rocks on which they trod made rumbling sounds.

Shenken was running, pursuing them up the mountain.

"He's a coward!" Enduli's feet were planted firmly on the rocks as he spoke. He felt that he had grown taller, and had in that instant become an adult. The words he used were those of an adult.

"We don't care about that old mother bear 'Amaha'! We'll kill two at once and just take them down to the market and sell them. We'll go to the public bath house and wash, then we'll watch a movie, go down to a restaurant and have a meal. We could even have a photograph taken. I have always wanted to have a photograph taken," Bieerdan said contentedly. He had studied up to middle school and his books had enriched his knowledge a great deal, but there was no way of telling that to people like Shenken.

"It would be great if we could go on a trip to Harbin. Would we be able to sell the bear for that much money?"

"Yes, we'd be able to. Afterwards, when we're there, we can have a look at everything, and maybe even go on an aeroplane."

They arrived at the peak. This was the northern side, with very few trees and very big rocks. Not one flake of snow had fallen here.

A bit further ahead was a precipice, and below that was the gorge. One could not see the water when looking down from the top, because the gorge was very deep. It seemed as though everything was fixed to the spot.

You could only hear the deep, dark sound of the water.

Shenken rushed forward to block Bieerdan and Enduli's path.

"I beg you, don't wound it. Let it give birth to the cub. It's going to be born soon." Shenken's chest was right in line with the boys' gun barrels as he walked steadily towards them, one step at a time. His face was as steady and unchanging as a rock, and his eyes were fixed straight ahead.

"This is no affair of yours. We want to kill two in one go!" Enduli's finger pressed down on the trigger.

"Get out of the way!" Bieerdan pressed the gun barrel into Shenken's chest. "Is this mother bear your old woman?"

In the blink of an eye, without waiting for a reaction from Bieerdan and Enduli, Shenken grabbed the two guns, held them for a second as if he had never seen guns as old as these before, and flung them behind him, without a sound, into the gorge.

"XXXX your mother!" Bieerdan cursed, pulling the hunting knife out from his waist.

Enduli also pulled out a hunting knife from his waist. All the energy in his body surged to the tip of his knife.

"You want to use knives with me? You two dirty swine don't know what you're in for!" Shenken tightened his belt. He did not pull out his knife, but merely stuffed a few pieces of dried roe deer meat into his mouth.

The two knives came closer together and a fierce battle ensued.

Shenken was chewing dried roe deer meat and grunting at the same time. He was easily as strong as a bear, time and again hurling Bieerdan and Enduli to the ground. He also knocked their knives from their hands. One knife could not be found again, and the other fell to the bottom of the precipice.

Enduli lay on the ground unable to move. The lower part of Bieerdan's face was covered with blood. His neck had been nearly pierced by a tree stump. His left leg hurt as if it were broken. He wanted to stand up but was not able to. He closed his eyes.

Shenken's deerskin clothes were ripped to shreds but he had not been wounded. But he was not proud of his triumph. His face was as serious as before, and he continuously stuffed dried roe deer meat into his mouth. He felt that to throw Bieerdan and Enduli to the ground unarmed was something extremely natural, like a tree growing on the mountain, or a bear living in a forest; as natural as a mother bear conceiving a cub, and as natural as his stuffing his mouth with dried roe deer meat, and as natural as breathing. Would anyone pay special attention to these things? Ever since men have been born, it has been like that. It has been that way for generations.

"Bear!"

Enduli's cry sounded as if it had been ripped out of him. He saw that the mother bear had leapt up, like a grass mound in a dark night, rushing out from behind Shenken's back. Shenken dodged to his right and yelled out, "You two run quickly! Bieerdan, Enduli, run quickly!"

The bear jumped at Shenken and missed, breaking a birch tree as thick in the middle as a bowl, in front of him. It got up in a rage, arching to the left and right, fanning the air with both its paws. It twisted its body around and charged again towards Shenken. Shenken was standing behind the birch tree which had been snapped, his hand gripping that flashing, glowing knife. His eyes narrowed, gleaming with the same light as the tip of his knife.

Bieerdan and Enduli could see the four limbs of the huge beast very clearly, the head like a millstone, the gaping mouth, the white froth on its mouth, the pair of reddening eyes. The sound of its breathing was very heavy, and the beastly smell of bear emanated from its body.

In that second the bear jumped and missed again. Shenken leapt behind it, but had not landed on his heels when it charged towards him. Shenken was crushed by it. Just then the bear let out an ear-splitting howl—shrill and brutal. Blood spurted out from below its ribs, spraying out widely. It spilled out, reddening the snow, from which steaming froth arose.

Shenken embraced the bear tightly. The bear was struggling, and starting to roll over on the ground. The stones rolled around with it. Bieerdan and Enduli stared as Shenken and the bear rolled over the cliff together. The falling rocks which followed their bodies sounded like rain.

The whole thing only took a few minutes. Now it was totally quiet. The whole mountain peak was tranquil, as if it were looking for something. On the ground, apart from the patch of bear's blood and the grass that the bear had flattened, there was nothing. There was not the slightest trace left of Shenken.

The wind ceased. The sun dropped over a distant mountain, like the face of a glowing mirror.

Neither Bieerdan nor Enduli said a word, and neither looked the other in the eye. They walked silently together towards the gorge.

The gorge was very broad. Rocks the size of an ox's head were everywhere. At the foot of the mountain were a few scattered trees, whose leaves were still green. In the early autumn, the river was very narrow, as narrow as the sinew of a deer that has just been skinned. The surface of the river was tranquil. The sound of gurgling water came from the valley, showing that the river was still flowing.

Shenken and the bear lay by the side of a tree. Below their bodies were reeds whose flowers had already been blown away.

Shenken and the bear were dead. They were still hugging each other tightly.

Bieerdan and Enduli were sweating all over before they finally managed to separate them. Shenken still grasped a piece of bear fur tightly in his hand. They could not pull his fingers apart. The knife had pierced the bear under its ribs; even the handle of the knife had plunged through. The knife had entered very cleanly.

Shenken's face looked as if he was still chewing dried roe deer meat. It was very still, without the slightest trace of fear or sorrow.

Enduli pulled the knife out and wiped it clean on the bear's body. He walked towards the foot of the mountain. Shortly afterwards, he carried back two straight and smooth birch poles on his shoulder.

Bieerdan took his deerskin clothes off, and covered Shenken's wounds. He stood there silently, ignoring what Enduli was doing. It was the first time he had seen a person die, let alone so heroically. He thought that Shenken should not have died, he should have returned to the village. In their village, Shenken alone had slain a bear without a gun.

"The two of us can make a stretcher," said Enduli, carrying over a bundle of willow branches.

"We must remember to go and give the message to the girl Wurina," said Enduli.

"I won't forget. We will sever the bear's head to give to her also."

"There's his knife, too."

From far away in the valley came the cry of birds, white and circling high; and all below was spray.

Bieerdan and Enduli lifted Shenken onto the stretcher, then tied on the severed bear head and its gall bladder and carried it on their shoulders. Following the gorge, they slowly headed out of the mountain. The shadows from the setting sun stretched out across the landscape.

The two boys were very reticent. They uttered not a word; there was only the sound of stones crunching underfoot.

They walked for a long time. The shadows of the two walls of the huge mountain completely engulfed them. The road in front of them was still longer than the road behind them. It seemed as though they could walk forever and still not emerge from the gorge.

"Enduli, how do you feel?"

"You mean the weight on the stretcher?"

"Yes."

"I think it's very light," Enduli said.

"I think it's very light too. It seems like there's not even the slightest weight on it."

They stood still, simultaneously and spontaneously feeling for Shenken on the stretcher. Their faces became disturbed and perplexed.

"He's still there."

"Yes, but how is it that there's no weight?"

They kept on walking, as if the road underfoot was becoming easier to travel.

"I want to die as Shenken did," said Enduli.

"I want to die like that too, but I—" Bieerdan—this young man who had attended middle school—stopped for a second, and heaved a long sigh saying, "But I don't want to live like he did."

"He lived with integrity," Enduli said.

"He hadn't even been to Harbin."

"No, he spent his whole life by himself."

"I really don't want to be by myself. I want to find a city girl."

The two were silent again. The more they walked, the lighter the weight on the stretcher seemed to be. It seemed as though they were walking along with no burden. Even the two birchwood poles weighed nothing.

"Have you heard before that people have souls?" Enduli broke the silence.

"I've heard that, but I don't believe in souls," Bieerdan said in a very confident tone.

"The souls of Shenken and the bear have been left on Lele Mountain, and that's why they feel really light to us."

"You mean, the soul is the heaviest part of someone?"

"Yes. Why else would our stretcher feel so weightless?"

They disappeared into the darkness, harboring an unspeakable sadness.

Yellow Smoke
Translated by R. Davis

I first heard this story at a Russian friend's house. He was leaning against the wall by the fireplace chewing wine-soaked Mahe tobacco, his eyes gazing steadfastly at the door. The pauses between each sentence were very long, as if he was using all his energy in telling the story. His whole body was shaking, so much so that in the end he couldn't continue. Later at the Huma'er River, I again heard the same story told by a boat captain. The two of us were snuggled under the same blanket. That night there was a huge snowfall; we couldn't even hear the sound of the waves of the Heilong River. After that, I heard two Oroqen hunters talking at a bus depot eighty miles from Tugen. Everyone was gathering around the fire, drinking warmed wine. It was a particularly long night. Before the story had been completely told, the two hunters and a few of the bus owners started an argument, and knives were drawn. Many years after this, I returned with a geographical investigation unit from the Harbin Social Science Academy to the area where the story took place, in order to investigate the tale. Mount Taerdaqi was spewing greyish brown lava all over the vegetation. There were practically no trees left; the fearsome, mighty ancient forests were no more. At the summit of the mountain was a round lake. The deep water was as clear as jade, so clear it appeared blue, and an atmosphere of mystery prevailed. This was the lake where they had discovered the strange beasts which were reported in the newspaper.

A mist, heavy as a rock, pressed down on the treetops. The branches of the trees creaked. The forest was pitch-dark, without a single ray of light. The sounds of coughing and of horses' hooves, continually rising and dying away, could be heard clearly. At midday the mist lifted. The edges of the forest were as clear as if there had only been light rain, but deep in the forest some remnants of mist lingered.

One by one, the cone-shaped *xierenzhus*, which were made of pieces of birchwood, were spread out along the grassy flats next to the river. The horses were scattered all around the *xierenzhus*, the dogs at their sides guarding them. In front of the *xierenzhus* were bushes of birch-leaf pears. They were dense dark trees, in disorder like a group of hibernating bears slumped in all directions. In front of these small bushes, women and children were kneeling on the ground, their faces buried in their hands, intoning a muffled chant. It was as if their hoarse heavy song was emanating from a crack in the earth; it sounded like a great steel ball rolling around the gorges. Gradually the song grew louder and more sonorous, until finally it screeched out like a screaming hurricane, full of insatiable longing. That longing could be seen in the eyes of all the women and children. They lifted up their heads, staring at the pine trees on the slope, transfixed with horror.

Far away, the pine forest on the mountain slope was dark. In the forest men were also kneeling; across their knees were firelock and *Bieladanke* rifles. They were chanting too. Their song went like this: "We have lived in these mountain forests from generation to generation; we are as one with the grass, the trees, the wild animals and the birds. Who is our grandfather? And our grandfather's grandfather? And our grandfather's grandfather's grandfather? Who was the ancestor of the dog-breeding and the deer-herding tribes? Do you hear us, O Heaven? Do you hear us, O Great Mountain?" They sang it over and over again, as if they had something on their minds, but also as if they weren't thinking anything at all. Each of the rough, rugged faces radiated a metallic glow.

They were waiting, waiting for a solemn and sacred time. Some of them were from very, very far away places. They had already waited for many days. From here, they would go on to their winter hunt. They gathered here every year before the winter hunt, bringing their most prized possessions to offer as a tribute to the god. It seemed as if they had been sitting here praying for many years. Their ancestors had never missed this event.

"Hey!... Oh! He's coming!" said a hoarse voice.

"Everyone look! He's coming! He's coming!"

Following this cry, which seemed to have split the trees in half, the chant stopped. Everyone blew the tinder on their fire and lit the joss sticks which were planted in a mound in front of them. The women and children all lay prostrate on the ground, not lifting even their heads. The men raised their guns above their heads and fired, aiming towards the heavens. Then they too lay prostrate.

At the front of the crowd, an elder stood up. He was holding the "Adamala," a birchwood box, with a myriad of decorative patterns burnt into its surface. It was he who had shouted that the god was coming. When they had been singing he had been the only one with his eyes open, staring confusedly at the wisp of yellow smoke rising from the mountain summit. The smoke spread and coiled around the tree trunks. It became amber coloured, growing thicker and thicker until it filled the forest completely. As thick as solid pine resin, it quickly ballooned until it reached the treetops, forming one cloud after another in the sky. These clouds rose quickly. Watching this the elder felt as if the mountain were moving too, as if his insides were being twisted around and torn to pieces.

He stood still. He didn't know what that smoke was, even though he had come here with his father and mother every year since he was small. Scores of times he had seen the mountain smoking, and had smelled that terrible rotten egg smell and seen an old man from their midst walk off towards the mountain, chanting, carrying the box filled with precious tribute, never to return again. But why was the mountain smoking? Why, from the time that the smoke had appeared, had there been fewer and fewer birds and animals on the mountain? Why had so many trees withered and died? Was this the god's punishment? Where did the god live? He was puzzled, but wanted one day to go to the place where the god lived. This was the concern of the old and the honor of being a father. His father had walked off towards the yellow smoke and never returned. Now, it was his turn.

He gazed at the thick smoke rising higher and higher from the summit. The misgivings on his exhausted face disappeared and in their place there appeared a dignified and holy expression. Tears spilled out of his eyes, and, intoning a wordless chant, he headed off towards the smoke.

During his hoarse song, all those lying prostrate raised their heads from the ground, nervously, quizzically but respectfully, watching his indistinct form as it slowly disappeared into the yellow smoke.

He was wearing the deer-head hat—the *Mitaha*—that his wife had sewn for him. It still had the eyes and ears intact. He also wore the golden deer-skin robe—the *Niluosusi*—and the elk-skin boots with cotton soles—the *Aoluqi*—that his wife had spent several months sewing. His back had gradually become stooped but his worn-out old legs could still carry him almost as fast as a young man's. Only his wife could hear his bones creaking. She put her hands over her face to muffle her sobs. The back of her neck was bent over like a bow, her shoulders hunched; hot, sweaty steam was rising from inside her collar.

When Zhebie was only a twelve-year-old child, kneeling beside Mother, he didn't know what sorrow or honor were. Neither did he know why people worshipped and prayed to the yellow smoke. He would never forget the sight of his family before they set off from Zhali River. They sat beside the charcoal fire, Father gulping wine, gazing confusedly at a statue of Bainaqia, the mountain god.

Zhebie's father hadn't wept. He couldn't. Yet Mother's hair had turned completely white on the road back from the mountain to their campsite by the river. Oh, heaven, how did she get like this? Was it because she didn't want Father to go to the god? Zhebie thought. But time after time, she said to him, "Your father has gone to the god. God is keeping him there. He'll never suffer again. He's a good man. His eyes are good, and he was still great with a gun, (truly—those eyes of his were as sharp as a cat's in the dark) but his legs had been broken twice so he couldn't ride. How much suffering he had borne... (She would talk and talk and then cry, using her wet hands to wipe her face, her eyes gleaming with a strange radiance). If he hadn't broken his leg, I could have given him another two sons." At the campsite beside the river they were the smallest family...

At that time Zhebie's mother was still very young. She wore a golden red *axisusi*, her forehead was fair, she had rosy-red cheeks. She always attracted the attention of men. Zhebie was still small; he didn't yet understand the intentions of adults.

Nine years later, Zhebie won the highest honor amongst his peers because of his great archery. He became the youngest and most famous horseman of his tribe. He was engaged to Gulayier's most beautiful but rather silly girl, Mowa, Namulun's third daughter, who was then only seventeen. When Zhebie brought Gulayier two buckets of beer, two wild pigs that he had hunted, and a pair of deer antlers, she rode off on her horse. Zhebie had to chase her onto Kuni Mountain. He found her in Bear's Ditch, with the river between them.

"Don't ride across the river!" she said from her mount, staring at Zhebie. From behind her she got out her bow and placed an arrow in it, saying, "I'll shoot an arrow to you. You have to catch it and then cross the river. I'll be waiting for you in the birch forest."

"Make sure that you don't hit me in the eye and blind me! Then I won't be able to see what you look like and how plump your legs are." He took off his leather hat and covered his eyes.

"Watch the arrow!" Mowa shot, then without turning her head she galloped towards the birch forest on the mountain slope. The river banks echoed with her laughter.

"Good shot!" Zhebie concentrated on the sound of the arrow's whistle. He plucked the arrow from the air and put it in his hat. It was a whistling arrow that Mowa had made. Twined around the shaft was a piece of red silk, and on the piece of silk she had embroidered her name. He spurred the horse on and forded the river, making his way into the birch forest.

The further he went into the forest, the denser it became. Zhebie jumped off the horse. He still hadn't seen Mowa when he heard her singing:

Fine threads of deer ligaments are tightly joined together,
The embroidered flap of my tunic is open,
Oh my love, where are you?
Making me wait till my tears have run dry.

Zhebie's song answered hers as he caught sight of her red dress. He sang as he walked towards her:

The hunter leaves the village enclosure and goes a thousand miles away,
I've left my shadow with you,
Grit your teeth and wait for me, my love,
I'll bring back deer antlers for you...

Zhebie had not finished his song before Mowa scurried up to him like a fawn.

"Don't you want to look at my face?... Hey! No touching, you're only allowed to look," she teased him.

"Your eyebrows are really dark."

"Do you want to look at my legs?"

"Everyone says that you are a good woman only if you have plump legs. My mother's legs are very plump..."

"Then I'll take my pants off and show you but you can only look from behind and you must stand a long way off."

Zhebie was a little nervous, as if his finger was on a trigger waiting for his prey to come closer. He suddenly felt as if his eyes had misted over. In front of him was only a white light, like a patch of snow.

"You're really stupid!" said Mowa laughingly as she ran her hand through Zhebie's tousled hair.

Their eyes met as she said, "What are you doing standing there like an idiot? Don't you like my legs?"

"No...I was thinking, I have to go away. After I'm gone what will you do?"

"Where are you going? To Black River to look for gold?"

"If you want a pair of bracelets, I'll go there."

"Are you going to Wulagan?"

"No, I want to go to the place where the god is. I probably won't be coming back."

"You're going to...Taerdaqi? You're mad! Is that really where you're going?"

"I've been thinking about this for a long time, waiting to talk it over with someone."

"Am I that someone?"

"My mother said, if I must go, I must first give her a grandson..."

Mowa lowered her head as he added, "I'm not commanding you but if I really don't come back, please look after my mother for me."

"Why are you going there anyway? The god must want to keep you," Mowa said, her eyes filling with tears.

"I don't believe the god lives there. Have you ever thought that it could be an evil mountain spirit? Otherwise, why are all the birds and animals around here gradually leaving? Why is the god always punishing us? I haven't forgotten the look in my father's eyes that evening, just before he went up the mountain. He was a *Mukunda*. He had been away to study. He had suspected that there was no god in the place where the smoke came from, but he didn't want to disobey the will of the tribe."

"You shouldn't be suspicious. You'll have to be like your father. In a few years you'll be a *Mukunda* too."

"My father probably wants me to go to the mountain top and bring back news from the place he's gone to. That is likely to be his wish."

Zhebie pulled the arrow out of his hat, broke it with a snap and put the tail in Mowa's hand. He held her hand and said, "Don't worry about me. If I don't go, the people of the campsite will always want someone to go and find out if there really is a god at Taerdaqi Mountain and if the yellow smoke really does come from it." When he had finished speaking, he mounted his horse and rode off down the mountain.

Three days later they had again pitched tent at the foot of the mountain. The *xierenzhus* were put up beside the river, and the horses were scattered along the river flats. Everyone was kneeling, and chanting. Zhebie was hidden in the birch forest on the mountain slope. He had a knife with him to use when he got to the mountain top. He was kneeling but he wasn't chanting. He was thinking: are my tribe and the bear really descended from the same ancestor? Is the mountain god a bear?

Zhebie's mother did not dare come out of her *xierenzhu*. She was kneeling on a white felt rug. The news that her son was going up to look for the god had spread around the cluster of tents like a bad omen. Some people had sprinkled snake blood and thrown wild pigs' hooves on her front door. She had cried so much that she had seen none of this. On the night before he left, she grasped her son's hand, saying, "If you are still determined to go to the mountain top, I will die there too." She still thought that this was the god's will, and she also had a knife hidden in her bosom.

Most sorrowful of all was Mowa. She never said another word to try to dissuade Zhebie from going up the mountain. Nor had she seen him again.

That day, at Neiersu Gorge, she had stopped Zhebie on his way back from hunting. Grabbing his robe, her bosom swelling, she was so excited that she could hardly stand still: "Everything is ready, Zhebie, the blanket that we'll use, the child's clothes, the dried deer meat that I'll eat, and the wine... Let me give you a child. I'm your woman, I can give you a child! I can!"

"Mowa, do you want to destroy me?" Zhebie knocked her to the ground with his fist. "Our ancestors said that the god will not speak to men who have slept with a woman and that such men will never be able to return to the world again."

"But what will I do? I can have your child! I can! Zhebie, I'll take my clothes off. Try me, I can have your child!"

She really did take off her clothes...but Zhebie didn't even look at her; he just got on his horse. She ran across and held his horse, crying and shouting, "If you don't want me, I'll die here!"

She took the knife out from Zhebie's waist, driving it towards her chest. Zhebie grabbed her but the knife had already pierced her collar bone and she fell.

Zhebie bound her wound and took her back to her *xierenzhu*. Later, he quietly rode away, leaving the campsite by the river, never to see her again.

Mowa knew that all men were just as cruel-hearted; they didn't understand women. If a man had something that he had decided to do, the best thing that a woman could do was not say anything. So long as you could let him take your heart with him, then it was all right. Her father had gone to the place of the god, the year before last. The god had kept him there; he had never returned. Her mother had cried so much that she almost turned to water. She had gone away and died. Now who would pity Mowa?

Everyone began slowly intoning the wordless chant, but Mowa did not sing or close her eyes. Instead she stared at the birch forest. Her heart knew where Zhebie was hiding. She saw him! His shape. It was black in contrast to the light from the mountain. It was as if a light blue flame was dancing on Zhebie's roeskin hat.

The mountain suddenly appeared very alive and young. After the mist had lifted you could see the curl of yellow smoke rising among the black trees. "He's coming! Look everyone, he's coming! He's coming!"

Zhebie kept staring, but he could see nothing but the yellow smoke. His whole body was trembling; he couldn't stop his teeth chattering. That yellow smoke kept him waiting a long, long time. It was as if he was still inside his mother's womb, waiting until this moment to be born. He leapt up suddenly, running straight towards the summit.

The elder at the front of the crowd dropped the birchwood box. The people were stupified. They watched, terrified, as Zhebie passed the statue of Bainaqia, carved into the pine tree, and continued walking towards the smoky mountain top.

Mowa's heart was thumping as if it would burst. She stood up, her two hands holding the broken arrow to her breast.

"Shoot your arrows! Kill him!"

The crowd didn't know who had shouted out. There was a sound of arrows being pulled out of quivers and of rifle bolts being readied. But Mowa ran towards the summit as if crazed, crying out, "Don't shoot! Don't shoot!"

She ran up to the front of the crowd, thinking that she would use her body as a shield against the arrows and bullets, but before she stopped running a bullet hit her and she fell.

Among the whistling of bullets and arrows, the leaves fell like drizzling rain and scattered all over Mowa's body and, far in the distance, over Zhebie's path.

The mountain was suddenly silent. The gunmen and archers could see that their fire wasn't reaching Zhebie. He was like a snow fox as he scurried along, disappearing in the thick smoke.

Zhebie didn't take any notice of the firing behind him, or even of Mowa's cries. He was conscious only of the blunt knife (it was the same knife that had entered his mother's chest and Mowa's collar bone) cutting little by little into his heart. Blood flowed from the wound, soaking his robe, flowing down his trousers and into his boots. So that he seemed to be stepping in puddles, and the blood make a gurgling sound.

The noise seemed very distant, as if it were coming from the belly of the mountain. He was surrounded by smoke, yellow smoke. He couldn't see a thing. It was as if he were lost in a labyrinth. He was gripped by terror, not knowing what was in front of him. If he took another step forward he would probably fall into the abyss of hell his grandmother had told him about.

He struggled forward, taking one large and then one small step. Suddenly, he noticed that the smoke all around him was gradually getting hotter, as if he was walking into a fire or entering a warm dream world.

He must have reached the top of the mountain. The smoke wasn't as thick here as it had been on the road, but that rotten egg smell was so bad it was like being in a gunpowder pit. Every stone that he stepped on was scalding hot; the smoke was hissing out of crevices in the rock.

One by one, amongst the mess of stones, he discovered dead bodies. Some were lying face upwards, some were trying to push their hands into a rock crevice; other bodies were twisted, with hideous faces, as if they had put up a frightful struggle before dying; still others had curled up into a ball, baring two incomplete rows of yellowing teeth... They were the men who had been offered as sacrifices to the smoke. They had been destroyed by vultures and wolves. No part of their flesh remained untouched.

It was like a battleground here. Had they fought a fierce battle against the god? Or had the god taken their souls away, letting the vultures and wolves have their fill? Zhebie found the corpse of his father. He was under a withered pine tree, half-sitting, half-squatting. He couldn't tell whether the vultures and wolves had been at him or if he had ripped open his own chest, since his two blackened hands still grasped the two sides of flesh.

It was then that Zhebie lost all sense of reason. He was like a man who had really gone mad as he chopped tree branches, raked up stones and buried each corpse.

While he was raking up the stones, he realised that a gurgling sound was coming from underneath the boiling rocks. His hands were ground down and charred by the rocks, but he wasn't aware of it. He continued to rake the stones. He didn't know how long he had been doing it, but he had also dug a hole big enough to bury himself in. The smoke and rumbling sounds were still coming up from under the rocks.

This was proof. But proof of what? He was so tired, he leant against a tree beside the great chasm to rest a while. Then, slowly and wearily he moved down the mountain. His face was as yellow as the smoke, but he was unaware of the pungent sulphurous smell. All he could see in front of him was his father's shrivelled and agonized face. He felt as if he were surrounded by pairs of wolves' eyes burning like green flames; vultures were wheeling and crying overhead.

At the foot of the mountain people were still kneeling, as if they were waiting for something. Later, he discovered that they were waiting for the the god's vengeance. Not one of them imagined that Zhebie would return. When they saw him they were dumbfounded. They knelt there, petrified.

Zhebie walked among them and stopped in front of the prostrate, bleeding Mowa. He discovered that his family's *xierenzhu* had been set on fire. He guessed that his mother must be dead. Their horses were lying in front of the pile of ashes.

"I found my father! I found my father!" He suddenly called out loudly. He didn't feel afraid. He had been a little afraid when he had set out, but now he didn't feel anything, only empty. He walked up to each of those kneeling, his blackened hands shaking: "I saw that the yellow smoke came from fissures in the rocks. I used my hands to break open rocks and saw that the smoke came from beneath them..."

No one moved—they were all looking at him, stupified. Regardless how loudly he shouted, no one took any notice of him. They didn't believe him.

The elder hobbled across to him, slapping him across the face, roaring, "Who believes your lies? You've brought disaster upon us!"

The people cried out in shrill voices and threw themselves at him. Glaring at him like hawks, they beat him to the ground.

It was a long while before astonishment and pain cleared from Zhebie's head. He suddenly got up from the ground and pulled out his knife, twisting it in his hand saying, "I didn't die on the mountain and I'm not going to die at your hands. I spoke the truth. I wouldn't lie to you. I really didn't see anything. I saw only the smoke coming from the fissure..."

"Cut out his tongue! What are you waiting for?" came the elder's shrill cry.

It was hard to count how many knives were drawn against Zhebie, the moonlight illuminating them and making them glint coldly. Zhebie didn't understand why they were acting like this towards him. He could see that they were very angry and ashamed. His heart felt unusually calm as he looked at the familiar, but cold, eyes. In an instant those eyes had become distant and strange, as if the stars in the sky had floated away down the river.

The yellow smoke still drifted across, covering the trees on the summit, spreading above the crowd's heads and causing the dark, hard faces to become distorted and indistinct.

"Use your knives!" the elder yelled.

Zhebie distinctly remembered this old man spearing fish and hunting fox with him, telling him the legend of Maokaodaihan and the story of Baigalashan by the campfire when he was small. He had taught him to sing:

I'm not afraid of snow on the Xing'an mountains,
I have a pair of leather boots,
I'm not afraid of hail on our tent roof,
I have a gold embroidered leather overcoat.

Before Zhebie could finish thinking this or look again at the old man's rock-hard face, there was a flash of light. One of them moved closer and he felt his face sting as a sharp steel edge cut into it. Again he was stabbed by a knife—this time in his arm. Zhebie waved his knife around in the air. Before he was able to make out who the attacker was that was closing up on him, Zhebie again felt a knife plunging into his ribs, in the same way that his father had taught him to kill bears. The knife edge turned inside him; he fell to the ground heavily.

As he was lying on the ground he heard the rumbling sound from under the rocks. His lips quivered slightly; he wanted to open his eyes and tell them. Again he heard it. Soon, he could think no more, he could hear no more... Silence. All Taerdaqi mountain was quiet.

Empty Mountain
Translated by J. Gondwe

Wurina had just emerged from the birch grove when she saw the man beside the water. He was the first person she had seen in six months.

Her left foot had been pierced by a splinter which had become partly imbedded. The old *Bieladanke* rifle slung over her shoulder rocked and swayed as she walked.

Her grandfather never allowed her to leave the *mukeleng* but she had sneaked out while he was branding at the lumber yard. Accompanied by a long-haired dog and a roe fawn which she had tamed by handfeeding, she made her way to the road that led down to the base of the mountain. Every day she went to the mountain road which had been used in the past for transporting lumber, but had since fallen into disuse. Hidden in a mountain birch tree, she would gaze at the darkened mountain pass and wait for somebody. She didn't tell her grandfather. In fact she did not know herself for whom she was waiting.

On the descent from the middle of the ridge, it was impossible to bypass the big spring. Day and night water from the cave gurgled, bubbled and brimmed over onto the adjacent meadow. Willows grew in profusion and flocks of water fowl flew up like thick clouds blocking out the sky. The spring was very shallow, never any more than waist-deep. It was extremely clear, tranquilly reflecting the color of the sky like a mirror.

The man was on the other side of the spring, under a wizened mountain elm. He had hung his clothes over an elm branch and stood naked in the water. Bending at the waist, he scooped up water in his hands to drink and sprinkled water over his arm. On his shoulder and thigh there were badly festering wounds. His muscular body glistened with ironlike lustre in the shimmering azure water.

"You can't drink the spring water," Wurina called out.

Her mouth was opened wide, yet no sound came. It had been such a long time since she had last spoken. She and her grandfather lived together. Each day was as repetitive and monotonous as the sun rising in the east and setting in the west; neither of them spoke. All that was necessary between them was an expression in the eyes or a single gesture of the hand. Words had become superfluous. As they watched over the mountain, the piles of timber in the woods, the already white *mukeleng* and the bear-fat lamp, neither of them could remember how long it had been since they last spoke.

The long-haired dog emitted a sound like the low whistle of the mountain wind in the withered tree branches. He couldn't bark like the hunting dogs at the base of the mountain. His was a sound from within the throat. He frequently turned his head to look at Wurina's eyes. His severed stick-like tail stood erect. The dog's tail had been cut short by her grandfather when it was just a few days old and too young to feel pain. Her grandfather said a dog with a severed tail could catch wolves.

The roe fawn, cowering with cold, had snuggled up against Wurina's legs. With its head protruding, its two small round eyes stared at the water. It limped on one of its legs. It had probably been wounded by a wolf one day when the snow had fallen heavily and had blocked up the door to the *mukeleng*. Wurina went out early in the morning and found that the roe fawn had collapsed in front of the wood heap. It was barely breathing and its body had become stiff.

Wurina stood there staring blankly at the man. She felt her throat blocked by something hot that made her whole face burn. It was the first time that she had seen such a healthy and strong man. Those glistening muscles, that tousled black hair, that silken velvet hair on his chest, made her feel as though she was grasped tightly by a large powerful hand. At first she felt a little frightened, but then her feelings changed gradually to become gentle and warm. She had never felt like that before. When she first came to the mountain she had been only a small child. She never ventured out. Even when her grandfather bathed her she felt a bit shy. Now she was twenty. The feelings that filled her heart bewildered and tormented her. She started to have strange dreams at night. Wurina felt as if the whole mountain was in turmoil in her heart. The sensation disturbed her and made her long to talk with someone so she could bare her soul. Each day she ran freely in the woods and each day she descended the mountain to wait. She sensed something unsettling there.

To her, all things were parts of a whole. Every tree, every rock and every blade of grass were at one with her.

Perhaps this was the person for whom she had been waiting. Otherwise why did his body seem to her to be glowing? The water, woods, grass and the whole sky all seemed to be dyed bronze.

Bang! She fired her gun.

The man, his body still dripping from the water, stood up. He stared at her in alarm.

"You can't drink that water! It's..." Wurina's voice quavered so much she couldn't speak.

The man ran to the withered elm, splashing loudly through the water as he did so. He hastily dressed and then made his way back through the stream towards Wurina.

He took large steps, but his progress was very slow. It was as though both legs were sinking into mud, although the bottom was sandy and hard.

Wurina could see his face clearly; it was scarred. His clothing was tattered and he looked like a fragmented rock. His eyes, however, glinted as brightly as the point of a knife. Under his gaze, Wurina's whole body trembled.

He suddenly fell, splattering forth a large spray of water. Several times he attempted in vain to climb out of the water. Eventually he regained his footing and Wurina ran over to support him.

"Are you one of them?" He didn't look at Wurina. He was staring at the spring.

"Whom do you mean?"

"They have chased me for three days and three nights. They rode horses. I saw their bastard of a leader at Black River Gold Mine. He suddenly turned his face and seized Wurina with his hands. "Did they give you money?"

"I don't know them." Wurina had no idea of events or happenings beyond the mountain.

The man narrowed his eyes and, standing close to Wurina, gazed at her.

She smelt his damp odor of sweat and tobacco. She felt his heavy breath and felt its hot gush against her face.

"You look innocent. I suppose you have never slept with a man before?"

"You...!"

Wurina was very scared. No one had ever spoken to her like that before. She had never had any idea of what she looked like. She stood stiffly, stock still. She felt that her whole heart had been shattered, smashed. Her whole body seared with heat as she flushed again. Without revealing the slightest expression of fear, anger or annoyance, she stared directly in front of her at that man who was laughing strangely.

The man thrust out his hand and seized the rifle slung across Wurina's back. "I can't let anyone know that I have reached this mountain! I can kill you or you can kill me, but I don't want to fall into their hands again. I don't want to let those bastards drag me on the street and ridicule me."

He forcefully seized the rifle and fell into the water again. The rifle was flung from his grasp into the water. The wound on his leg was very deep; blood was darkening the water.

Wurina helped him up again. They didn't look at each other as they chose the smoothest path and made their way up the mountain.

Although she was extremely familiar with that heavily wooded mountain, it still held a great deal of mystery for her. Every year snow began to fall in September and didn't melt until May the following year. Then the sound of water was heard everywhere and the grass and trees became dark green overnight. All night and all day the mountain was hidden in a green fog. The wind was fragrant and carried with it every imaginable sound. Living in such a place, you would be buffeted by all kinds of sounds that made you feel overwhelmed and soothed, agitated and serene, lonely and excited.

The sun was very, very far from them. In winter and summer it looked down upon them like a tranquil eye. Possibly there were no other people on the mountain, apart from Wurina and Grandfather.

His arm pressed heavily on her shoulder and the further they went the heavier the pressure became. For the first time Wurina found the mountain path long, and it was as if she could not even recognize it.

"Who else is on the mountain?" The sound from his throat was deep, like the turbid rumbling of thunder.

"My grandfather... There's just the two of us." The pressure bearing down on her shoulder made her unafraid.

Beads of sweat rolled down the man's stone-like face. Blood from his wound flowed down his trouser leg. Because Wurina's foot had been immersed in water, her wound started to sting hotly, searing into her. Neither uttered a sound. They were each engrossed in their own thoughts.

The man toppled to the ground when they reached the front of the *mukeleng*. Wurina sat beside him and looked at him. His eyes glinted as he watched her. His gaze caused her whole body to flush hotly, so that she didn't even notice her aching foot.

All around, it was still.

The sound of the wind could be heard in the woods. From there, the woods looked dark black. There was a small path that had been trampled flat beside the wood from which one could pass into the timber depot. Year in, year out, her grandfather kept watch over the piles of timber. All the thick, old yellow pine trees had been felled from the mountain field when her grandfather was young. Grandfather said it had been fifty years or so. But he didn't really know how many years had passed. Young trees already a foot or more in diameter had grown in the previously felled forest. During the rainy season it was filled with pine mushrooms that nobody picked. They rotted, only to regrow with the next fall of rain.

Her grandfather came walking along the ecru path. He still wore the sleeveless jacket from those years when he felled timber. It was made from moose leather and over the years it had worn so that not a hair remained. Although he cherished the jacket lovingly and took meticulous care of it, it had many holes. He had mended them himself with deer sinew. In one hand he carried a charcoal fire and in the other a long iron rod with a figure "+" on its point: an iron brand. It glowed red hot in the charcoal fire.

Her grandfather's job was to brand every log with the mark "+." Every day he went up the mountain to brand. Every tree trunk had been branded, some of them several times. However, he still persevered until the day that the timber would be transported down the mountain.

"It won't be long," Grandfather always said, "they will be here soon." Later he heard that his old workmates had died one by one, even Laoqutou from the train station who had despatched them to the mountain to fell timber.

Apart from he himself who guarded the timber piles, there was no one else. It was during one such night that he suddenly lost the hearing in one of his ears. Although he never said "It won't be long" again, he still believed firmly that one day the timber would eventually be transported. He just couldn't bring himself to think that the timber would just rot on the mountain.

"This pile of timber represents two years of felling. One fellow was crushed to death by a falling tree; he wasn't even of marriageable age. Another was savaged to death by a bear. Another froze to death. Three dead, four more wounded. At that time we numbered more than a hundred."

Every time Grandfather walked past those four weed-covered graves, he would stand silently for a while shaking his head, and sighing he would say, "They were all buried wrapped in birch bark. After living a whole life they couldn't even get a few boards of pine. That Laoqutou. It's easier to squeeze piss out of a toad than to get wood out of him. It's difficult to clear up official business. For the first few years Laoqutou would come and look at piles of timber and those few graves. Afterwards he contracted hemiplegia and couldn't move. When he died he didn't even send a message. Perhaps he was able to obtain a few pine planks."

"Everybody forgot you long ago!" On one occasion Wurina could simply bear it no longer and blurted it out. But she had not intended to hurt her grandfather.

"You mean they've forgotten this pile of timber?" He didn't believe what his granddaughter had said.

In those years, a document with an official red seal had come to assign them the job of felling trees. Laoqutou had read it out aloud to everybody. Otherwise, why would he have been despatched to guard the depot? The pile of timber was all genuine, high quality yellow pine.

"On the third of the month, Laoqutou came running up and told us that in a few days there would be a train." Whenever Grandfather opened his mouth it was always to speak of things that had happened twenty years ago.

"Which year was that?"

"On the mountain there is no difference between the passing of one year or the passing of many. Time is moving for you. For me, it has stopped."

"Grandfather, will we live on this mountain all our lives?"

"Don't you like living on the mountain?"

Wurina didn't say anything else. Grandfather would not leave the pile of timber and she would not leave him. The pile of timber would not leave the mountain. This was their whole world...

Grandfather was approaching.

The man heard but didn't turn his head. However, he seized his short knife as he heard the footsteps.

"Put that knife down! My rifle has got eyes." Grandfather spoke from a long way off. His eyes were still as sharp as they were when he was twenty. The man threw the knife down.

Grandfather set down the rod and the charcoal fire and picked up the knife. He weighed it in his hand saying, "Good steel." He drew near the man. "Laoqutou from the train station also had a knife as good as this. He lost it the day of the first fall of snow. This made him fret the whole winter as if he were plagued by an evil spirit. For thirty days he didn't even have an appetite for mushroom dumplings. After a couple of nips of wine he was drunk and he vomited in my room."

"Grandfather, you are talking about the past again!"

"My knife was made for me by my friend on the gold mine. It has never drawn blood." The stranger looked at the old man with a cold, sidelong glance.

The old man walked up to the stranger and staring at him hard said, "You must've had those wounds for some time. They are festering." Saying that, he stuck the knife into the charcoal fire.

"What are you doing?" The stranger watched Grandfather with apprehension and, propping himself with his arms, sat up.

"I am going to remove the festering flesh with the knife, otherwise you will never leave this forest. You will rot on the mountain."

The stranger's expression immediately changed. He lay prostrate on the ground and kow-towed to the old man.

The old man blew on the charcoal fire and without even bothering to look said, "What I say counts on this mountain, except there aren't very many rules. If you are a man, uncover your wound and let me have a look."

The stranger took off his jacket and uncovered the wound on his shoulder blade.

"It's three to five days old; it isn't a cat scratch, is it?"

"It's a knife wound."

"You've really got balls, young man."

"The mounted troops were chasing me. That bastard of a leader was chasing me for a pound of opium. A pound of opium! I am worth a pound of opium!"

With a forced smile he asked the old man for a handful of tobacco. Putting it in his mouth he began to chew. "I shot that bastard. It's a pity it was in the leg."

"Where's your gun?"

"I chucked it; there were no more bullets."

The old man didn't ask anything more. It was as though he didn't need to. Everything was as natural as a tree shedding leaves. He smoked as he turned the knife in the charcoal fire. After a while he straightened up and said to Wurina, "Go inside, we've got men's business to attend to."

Wurina carried the roe fawn and entered the *mukeleng*. The long-haired dog did not move but remained close to the side of the charcoal stove.

Outside, they began operating on the wound with the knife. Wurina hugged the roe fawn tightly to her bosom. She wanted to stick close to the window and observe but she didn't dare look. She felt so flustered that it seemed her tongue was obstructing her throat and choking her. "Ahhh—!" Suddenly a hoarse, piercing cry came from outside. The drawn-out cry reverberated for ages on the quiet, still mountain. It was as if everything—the mountain, the trees, the room—had been split open for a moment. Wurina felt that she too had been cleft by the sound.

She awaited the second hoarse scream, and visualized her grandfather digging out the festering flesh of the man's wounds with the heated knife. She waited for the next scream, until her grandfather came inside. It never came.

"Go and help him on his way." Grandfather sat leaning against the wall on a wooden block, smoking.

"Can't he stay for a few days? I don't think he's a bad man. Let him go once his wounds have healed."

"No one can remain on the mountain. With that pile of timber, I won't be able to relax."

"Grandfather!..."

That damned timber! Wurina wanted to say something else but she saw Grandfather's expression and held back her words.

The wind rose in the woods. Leaves drummed against the glass window like raindrops. Grandfather knocked the ash from his pipe and packed it again with tobacco. He gazed at Wurina for a long time and said, "All right. Let him recover for a few days in Squirrel Cave. Carry over some dried venison, some wine and a grass mat for him."

Wurina gazed excitedly at her grandfather, then slowly stood up and went to go outside. She had completely forgotten the roe fawn that she had been clasping to her bosom. It fell to the ground, white foam gushing from the corners of its mouth.

"It's dead," said Grandfather.

"I smothered it." Wurina picked the roe fawn up again and cuddled it. She didn't understand how she could have killed it. It hadn't made a sound. That small thing!

"I couldn't bear his screams."

"He's a real man. That knife wound was to the bone."

"What made him come running here?"

"I don't like to ask about other people's business. Nor should you."

Wurina put the roe fawn on the ground and said, "Dying is so easy."

"Sometimes it is very difficult."

Grandfather came over and helped Wurina pack the things. He stuffed a pouch of tobacco leaves into the deer-skin bag.

The sky was already darkening as Wurina and the man followed the worn pale path up the mountain. The dog ran in front. The man carried the deer-skin bag on his shoulder. He didn't use her for support, nor did he speak.

The night fell, covering the mountain with a mesh of fog. The forest was extremely dark. A layer of mottled green mist floated on the tree-tops. Above the green was a layer of yellow, leaping like fire; the rocks were black, with an aura of insipid faint blue light.

Although the man never turned, Wurina felt that he had eyes all over him, all staring at her with a burning gaze that troubled her deeply. She felt that the entire forest was permeated with the essence of the man's breath, sweat, tobacco and wounds.

"Rest in this mountain cave for a few days. Nobody apart from Grandfather and me knows about this cave." Wurina lit a fire for him and squatted beside it. Dried branches and twigs exploded as she fed them to the fire, and tongues of flame leapt up to lick her face.

The man, reclining on the grass mat beside the fire, used his knife to pare a piece of dried venison. He then placed it in the fire, roasting it until tender and then put it in his mouth and chewed it. His even teeth flashed white and his narrowed eyes rippled faintly with amusement. He looked her up and down, without emotion, and regardless of anything Wurina said, he would not answer.

Wurina suddenly became frightened. She felt the man's hand extend towards her from the fire and stroke her hair, her cheek and her chest. She didn't dare move; no one had caressed her like that before. It seemed as if his hand was pressing down on her body, forcefully pressing down until she couldn't draw breath. That large hand slid over her body, moving downwards... ...She cried out in fear, "Don't...don't do that!..."

"What's wrong with you?" The man stopped slicing meat with the knife in his hand.

"Me...?" Wurina broke out in a cold sweat.

The man seemed to understand something, smiled, sat down and said, "Don't be worried about me. I have my knife and I won't let them take me alive, just to be exchanged for some crude opium."

Wurina was worried about herself and was frightened of her own feelings. But she wanted to feel them again. She needed to. She dropped her head in embarrassment. Using a pine branch she stirred the fire and said, "Tell me, why did you come running here?"

The man lay down, gazing at the cave roof, which was illuminated red by the fire. He said, "I am trying to hide from disaster. Actually, damn it, people can't hide from anything. We have a destiny in life and nothing can be avoided."

"Why do they want to chase you?" she asked.

"I can't tell you that right now."

"What if I want to know right now?" she persisted.

"Have I asked you anything?" he returned.

"Don't you want to tell me?"

"If you really want to know, come back to the cave in three days and I will tell you then."

Wurina stood up and added some more sticks to the fire. She stared boldly at him, then turned and walked out of the cave.

It was very bright outside. The moon had come out.

Grandfather's timber depot was not far from the mountain cave. When one gazed at it from a distance, it looked like a group of wild animals hiding in the forest. From watching over that group of wild beasts, Grandfather had already become old, the white hair on his temples creeping towards the crown of his head.

When she returned to the *mukeleng* and was making the bed for Grandfather, he suddenly blurted out, "Granddaughter, this man seems to have troubled you."

"He is really likeable. His body is attractive to me." Wurina had her back to her grandfather. Even she herself didn't know why she said it, but when she spoke she was very calm. It was as if the man had become part of her heart.

"I understand." Grandfather lit his pipe, engulfing himself in a fog of smoke. He was silent for quite a while before he said, "Because of that timber pile, I can't allow any one else on the mountain. If you want to go with him, then you go. I know I can't keep you."

"Grandfather, why are you talking like that?" she demanded.

"Your grandfather won't go anywhere as long as that pile of timber is here."

"Then I won't go either."

"But that man can't stay on the mountain."

"No, I know that. But he said... He told me to come and look for him after three days."

They didn't say any more. They were silent all night, though neither of them slept.

They could hear bird calls in the woods. There was one call that they had never heard before. The sound was long and drawn out but sweet and agreeable to the ear. It was like an ancient folk song. Sometimes the bird call was so close to Wurina it might have been on the window. The bird sang all night: "Slender girthed chestnut horse, could be worth eight hundred yuan; my beloved Guliehaote at the very most is worth eight fen...'

Grandfather kept on tossing restlessly, and he also coughed continuously. He cursed, "That bird's call isn't good, evil creature! It's like a wolf carrying off somebody's child." He gave a long sigh and then fell silent again.

Three days passed like this. For three days they didn't speak, not even at mealtimes.

On the afternoon of the third day, Grandfather helped Wurina pack the deer-skin bag and saw her out of the room.

"Come back at night fall. I will be waiting for you on the road."

"I know," she said.

The long-haired dog raced ahead, and although Wurina ran until her whole body was soaked with sweat, she couldn't keep up with it. Everything on the mountain seemed so cool, clear, bright and open. She hummed the night-bird's folk song, "How I loath to forsake you Guliehaote, you are constantly in my heart; I never see him come to visit me, maybe he is a scoundrel!..."

After passing through two pine forests, the long-haired dog stood still and whined. They were still a considerable distance from the cave. The dog's low growl seemed to Wurina like a warning.

She threw the deer-skin bag aside and hurried towards the cave.

It was empty. Apart from the grass mat neatly rolled and standing upright to one side, and a pile of ashes, there was nothing there. White rays of light flooded into the cave and illuminated the pile of white ash. The whole cave was deathly white and quiet.

Wurina could tell from the pile of ashes that the damned man had left yesterday or possibly the day before.

She stood at the mouth of the cave leaning against a rock. In the sunlight, the whole mountain seemed to be white—a fearful, terrible white.

The long-haired dog drew her attention to a pine tree not far from the cave. Whimpering, the dog circled the tree, emitting a low whine.

Wurina saw a knife stuck in the tree. She brightened. She walked up to it and recognised the man's knife. The knife's elm-wood handle was well worn and had a line of characters engraved on it. Unfortunately she had no education and could not read them.

Was it his name? She pulled the knife out and turned it over again and again in her hand, looking at the knife wonderingly. She didn't understand. Why did he stick his knife into the tree? Was he leaving it for her?

Suddenly it dawned on her that the knife was meant to show her the direction in which he had gone.

Impulsively, she followed the path to which the handle pointed.

She searched the mountain for the rest of the day, but found no trace of the man. When she returned to the *mukeleng* it was already so dark that she could not make out the path. Grandfather was waiting in front of the *mukeleng*. Inside, the lamp was unlit. They rarely lit the lamp because Grandfather thought lamps were evil.

"He's gone. I knew that he wanted to go. The mountain couldn't hold him..."

Wurina burst into tears before Grandfather had finished speaking and, stifling her sobs, fled into the room. She hated that man!

Grandfather waited until her crying subsided before coming inside. He sat beside Wurina and stroked her hair with his large, branch-like hand, saying, "I saw the knife earlier on. He left that same night. He was afraid that we would sell him. People are the same as trees, nobody really understands anyone else..."

"He should have told me that he didn't intend to stay on the mountain," she said.

"He told you by leaving his knife behind. I tell you, I can't hold you here. If you want to go, then go. When I was young I was like that young man and travelled about a lot."

Wurina lay on the *kang* thinking back over the events of the last two days. She didn't know what the man had felt when he met her. How did he feel when she helped him walk along? What did he feel as he chewed the dried venison beside the fire in the mountain cave? Grandfather certainly seemed to know. Grandfather knew everything, but he didn't tell her. Perhaps Grandfather had driven the man away.

She felt feverish all over. She might have become a tree, a crooked gnarled mountain elm growing beside the water, buffeted by winds and rains, shaking under their force. She clutched tightly at the earth, clasping the rock, terrified of being uprooted. She was so tired, as if every branch was ready to snap. She was numb, feeling absolutely nothing.

Rifle shots awakened her.

The shots came from far away down the mountain; sporadic, muffled rifle fire. There was also a sound of horses; numerous, steadily retreating, pounding hoof beats.

The window pane was red, the whole room illuminated by a red glow. Even the decorative pattern on the panther skin nailed to the wall stood out in bold relief.

Grandfather wasn't on the *kang*! She dressed and ran out of the *mukeleng*. She felt dark, unfathomable terror. The timber depot was ablaze. Red tongues of flame, thirty feet high, were suddenly flashing and sparkling, flaring skyward. Thick columns of greyish brown smoke billowed from the blaze. It was as if a herd of gigantic beasts was stampeding from the fire, accompanied by the deafening sound of explosions bursting and crackling around it.

The whole mountain was brighter than day.

Following the worn old path, she ran in a daze to the timber depot. She saw her grandfather. Grandfather had draped himself with an old sheep skin and was going step by step into the blazing, billowing stack of timber.

"Grandfather! Grandfather—!" she screamed.

But Grandfather disappeared into the midst of the huge billowing blaze. Wurina madly barged into the fire but the wind, whirled up by the fire, pushed her out. She tumbled down on the grass.

She tried several times to dash into the fire but to no avail. Her deer-skin clothes were alight. She didn't understand what had happened below the mountain—what could possibly have brought fire to the mountain and caused it to burn so brilliantly and so very quickly.

She loved the mountain, she hated that man!

She stared woodenly at the fire. There were no tears in her eyes; they were full of blood.

But she hated that man!

The Wilderness Inn
Translated by E. Cole

In the moonlight he could see her grave from a distance; he would have found it even without the moon. He was only too familiar with this rambling and derelict graveyard. One year he ran away from the Rongyuan Goldmine and hid himself here for five days and five nights. Apart from the corpses themselves, he had eaten almost everything he could find.

Now he could smell the newly turned earth of the grave. His eyes penetrated the night more sharply than needles. He resented the bright moonlight that made the grave look crude, like a clod of earth pushed up by some burrowing worm.

This was her grave. He believed his eyes and trusted his judgement. That bastard hadn't even given her a headstone; it was as though she was just a dead dog. She had spent fifteen years with him but he never treated her well, not once. That man had no concept of how important women were to men.

He knew. But she had never belonged to him. The previous year he was recuperating in the courtyard behind the lorry station at Xiahekou. He had been attacked by a rogue bear on Mount Lao and had tumbled down the slope; he clung to his life but broke a leg. Then she came. She took the Hejishan Warehouse lorry and brought medicine and festive glutinous rice cakes. He saw then that she wouldn't live long. The two hollows of her eyes were shadowed and her eyes were devoid of any sparkle of light. Although she stayed with him that night and they were squeezed together in the same bedroll, he didn't touch her. He felt ashamed, as though he had wronged her in letting her become like this, all for his sake. She was as tired and over-worked as a thrashed-out sesame stalk. She spent a restless night in the bedroll, squirming like a fish. Her neck was bathed in sweat. He knew that she was crying but he said nothing. She was still so young. He and her husband were both over forty, but she was not yet thirty and hadn't borne children. They should have understood how to love a woman, that a woman did not just want a gold bracelet. Dawn broke and she was still huddled close to his body; she showed no sign of leaving the bedroll.

"You should go. The train will come in a moment and you should hurry back to Duangou before nightfall," he said, running his fingers through her hair.

"I want to go with you. Take me with you!" she cried.

She was so close and looked at him so intently it was as though he was being compelled at knife-point.

"I am one man, I have one horse and one gun. I just wander about the mountains; I don't have any shelter," he said.

"I want you, not shelter!"

Women are more stubborn than men. He couldn't remember clearly how he finally persuaded her to go. Now, he felt only regret. If he hadn't let her go she would still be alive. She would rest her head on his shoulder and sing to him:

Ah, red opium poppy on Kuerbin River,
Cruel Brother crossing Kuerbin River rejects me,
I endure so much suffering for you,
Yet my heart rejoices in such hardship.
If you must go, I go with you,
Do not so cruelly abandon me.

The moon shone behind him and threw his elongated shadow across her grave. It was so peaceful behind him; there was just a slight rustling sound, like water or the leaves of the trees in the valley. He was almost unable to tell which way the wind was blowing. He could only feel the earth moving beneath his feet, now rising, now falling. He didn't know when the straw hat which he had tied to the grave had blown away. She had woven the hat for him and he had worn it until the brim frayed and eventually it disintegrated. He looked around at the rough graveyard and the cold and gloomy oak forest. He felt inexpressibly sad and suddenly his eyes were shrouded with tears.

Where is that fellow now? He heard a gatherer of medicinal herbs at the grindstone say that this fellow had recalled all his shares in the Hejishan Warehouse and left with the money. At first he didn't believe the story, but the herb-gatherer was also from Duangou and had seen it with his own eyes. He also said that this fellow had acted this way because his wife had died.

This news made him forget the wine and food that he had just bought and he hurried off to Duangou that same night. Duangou was a large town—ten miles of paths wound around it. The house he sought was on a slope in Goudongtou. The wooden gates were tightly shut but the three rooms were so bare not even a scrap of cloth could be found in them.

There was a musty smell about the *kang*. The curtains were tattered and it seemed that a fire hadn't been lit in the room for many years. From the broken window one could see the quiet and desolate sands of the river below, the dirt road alongside it and the hazel wood. The river glittered in the sunlight. All was silent. The hidden recesses of the distant river sands were obscured by a deep blue fog. Every time he had come to Duangou he had waited for her in these recesses until it was dark. When it was dark that fellow would gamble at the Hejishan Warehouse; he too was avoiding the eyes of the town.

"Fugeng buried his woman and repaid his debts to a few of the town's families. Then he left." His companion looked at him grotesquely; warm garlic-laden spittle spluttered from his mouth.

"Didn't he say where he was going?" He was motionless and gazed fixedly through the hole in the window.

"No. When he was in the inn all he said was that someone would come looking for him after a couple of days and that the two of them had a debt to settle."

"He's talking about me." He turned his head suddenly, his eyes flashing dreadfully.

The other man took a few steps back. "Fugeng is pretty easily provoked..." he warned.

"We were at the Rongyuan Goldmine together."

"Oh—" The man's big mouth dropped open. He gradually shifted his gaze from the Russian-made gun in the other's hand and said guardedly, "If there's nothing more I'll go."

"If you've got something else to do, you can go." His tone was harsh and cold and he stared at him as he put his hand on the rifle barrel.

"No, there's nothing else." His companion sighed deeply and restrained the trembling of his parted legs.

"Do you know where Fugeng's wife was buried?"

"Er... She was buried at night. No-one in the town really knows."

"That son of a bitch!" Suddenly he guessed where she had been buried.

"Aren't you going to the inn to have a drink and something to eat?" The man was still trying to work out a way to leave but those eyes full of grief and anger held him to the spot like hooks.

"There's no need." He reached inside his coat and felt for a deer skin pouch. He pushed it over. "Buy me a barrel of wine and a bolt of calico."

"Do you want good wine and good cloth?" the other asked.

"If the money isn't enough I'll pawn the gun."

"I'm not talking about money. If you go to the shop at Goukou there's good wine there but it's further away and I'll need more time."

He rested both hands on his shoulders and said, "Don't let anyone else know that I'm buying them."

The man nodded and made off as if he were escaping. After dark he threw the wine and calico over the gates. He didn't dare enter the room.

He smoked a cigarette in the darkness of the cavernous room. He didn't stir at the sound at the gate. His gun had only one bullet. He was waiting for Fugeng. He knew he couldn't go far. Every pore on his body seemed to be open with expectation.

He went to find the grave when the sun was far in the west. He sent the wine and calico on to a wild and lawless inn on the bank of the Heilong River. It was actually a cellar left behind by the people who had erected the headstones in the early days.

They had been together there that first time. She had just married Fugeng. It was because he didn't have six taels of gold, but she had felt constant regret over the money. She had tried to kill herself on several occasions.

"Fugeng! Where are you, you son of a bitch?" he howled by the river's edge and in the rambling graveyard. But heaven and earth remained indifferent and gave no reply. An enormous anger and frustration seemed to constrict his whole body. He was angry with the stillness and coldness of the night. He took his gun and smashed it to pieces on a rock. If he could have smashed himself he would have done that, too.

He crouched on the ground on one leg and began to dig up the grave. The earth was not yet frozen and was quite damp. Waves of damp air, pungent and bitter, assailed him. A bird was calling in the distant oak forest. He knew it wasn't really a bird call. That kind of bird wasn't found here; it was only found on the Kuerbin River. Moreover this particular fish-catching bird had no cry. He had imagined the sound.

His hands were scratched numb. Blood flowed from his cracked and split fingernails. His arms were burning, and his throat was hot and hoarse. That bastard Fugeng had buried her very close to the surface and it wasn't long before he could feel a wooden board through the soil.

He had just buried her between two wooden planks. He saw the colour of her face and he was sure she hadn't been dead three days. The flesh of her face still retained some vitality and firmness; her mouth was not shut too tightly and her eyeballs had not yet sunken in. Perhaps she had known he was coming and waited for him. Impulsively he picked her up and his heart, which had been fluttering like a leaf in a gale, beat more quietly.

While he had been standing before her grave, he had not worked out how he would open her coffin and his whole chest tightened with perplexity and torment. He was afraid that at the moment he saw her he wouldn't be able to stand it. But that feeling passed in an instant. An inexplicable impulse urged him on and forced him to overcome the stupefying dizziness that threatened him. He could feel his teeth chattering, and his legs were stiff. He stared woodenly at Nouhaer Mountain far in the distance. He passed through the graveyard, which shimmered in the whiteness of the icy cold moonlight, through the forest and towards the river's edge. He felt as if the road beneath his feet was raised above the earth like a bridge. It was as though it were leading straight to heaven.

The river lay at his feet. Yesterday, when he had come, the wind off the river was quite ferocious and the water whistled and scurried like a mob of frightened horses. The black waves were taller than a man and this spray splashed his face. Now there was not a breath of wind. The bare and deserted beach was flooded with white light and the water was as still as his beloved.

When he carried her into the cellar his heart was stirred with remorse, anger and guilt, and the feeling that he had been wronged. He had desperately wanted to hurl himself into the river with her in his arms. He felt that he had never lived like a real person. He felt she could have made him a man, but he had missed the opportunity. The year after he had run away from the Rongyuan Goldmine, he had gone on a winter hunt with a band of Oroqens on Mount Lao and had received a pouch of money, returning wounded to Duangou. A light was on in her room but it was actually that dirty swine Fugeng who came out. He looked as though he had been drinking and his fur coat hung open to reveal a chest bathed in sweat. One hand clutched at his waist-band, the other held a gun.

"Ugh, aren't you dead yet, you cur? Where did you shoot off to? Do you want me to send you off to the mines?" Fugeng sneered.

"I've come to look for Dazhenzi. I have money now." He leant against a pillar and swung the pouch in his hands.

"Are you bloody crazy? Dazhenzi belongs to me. I paid six taels of gold for her!"

"You know we've been in love for some years—you bastard!"

"All right then, give me sixteen taels of gold and I'll open the door for you." The rifle bolt clicked as he cocked it back and he pressed forward step by step. "If you don't have it you'd better get lost. Don't dirty my place with your filth!"

He had neither gold nor a rifle, so all he could do was step backwards against the wooden gates. Even though he nearly lost his life twice, he never managed to get together the sixteen taels. But he did not want to go off with Dazhenzi illicitly and break his agreement with that swine Fugeng. Now he was left with nothing to say.

He kicked away the cellar door, bent over and carefully carried her inside. It was so dark it was impossible to see anything.

Most cellars of this kind were dug into hollows in the hillside next to the river. Regardless of the aspect of the hill, the cellar doors always faced south. These doors were very small and low, rather like a wild dog's lair. They were often overgrown with wild grasses and shrubs which made it difficult for strangers to find them. Yet inside his cellar it was very spacious. There was a *kang*, an earth stove, a large crock of water, various vats of pickled cabbage and places where salt, grain, horse fodder and firewood could be kept. The people who set the wooden rafts up and down the river would put up here for a few nights to eat, drink and warm themselves. When they left, all they had to do was to pay for what they had eaten, drunk and used for fuel. This was the golden rule of the Wilderness Inn. Whoever came could stay; they could come and go as they pleased. There was no innkeeper—business was run on an honor system. Regardless of whether they were escaping to the river or hurrying to the mountains, money wasn't much use here as far as they were concerned. When things were quiet on the river this inn in the wilderness had some busy times. But for the past few years things hadn't been going very well. It was impossible to find even a piece of dry firewood.

He put Dazhenzi's body on the *kang* and lit a fire on the ground at her feet. The damp twigs hissed as the blue flame gradually became red, then yellow and finally white, and illuminated the whole cellar. He squatted by the fire and threw twigs into it while he smoked a cigarette. He decided to use the wine to clean her body and the calico to bind her up tightly. He would buy a decent coffin and bury her in the Shandong section of the Xiahekou graveyard, because he had once heard her say that her ancestors were from Zhangdian in Shandong. He also wanted to erect a headstone for her. He had enough money since he had, as well, a sum given to him out of kindness by the fellows at the mine.

That son of a bitch Fugeng didn't understand that, in these parts, women are immortal. His face was red from the heat of the fire, and he looked as though he had been drinking. He regretted not killing Fugeng last winter, at the inn at Laoshantoudao ditch.

The innkeeper there had also done work at his gold mine. He was now doing quite well, growing some crops and dealing in livestock. As soon as Fugeng had entered the room, he had sat on his table, seized the bowl of wine from his hand and drunk it all down as if it were water (he had never been able to out-drink Fugeng, not even at the mine). He had turned the bowl upside down on the table and said to him, "If you're not a bit quicker in getting together those sixteen taels of gold, Dazhenzi might not be able to wait around for you much longer. That little wench has tuberculosis, and she can't have children either. I—"

He didn't know whether it was hostility or anger, but he pulled Fugeng off the table and threw him flat on the floor. He was surprised at his own strength. He flattened Fugeng's nose and then continued to beat him up outside the inn. The drinkers inside and even the innkeeper were all crying out, "Kill him! Kill him!" They were already excited by gambling and dog fighting and were enjoying this. But he had removed his foot from Fugeng's wrist. Although he could have done his worst, he decided not to. He would rather save up his sixteen taels.

As the fire burned, it became more vigorous and grew so warm that he took off his deer skin cape and bared his body. His chest and back were covered in scars and sweat.

He removed Dazhenzi's clothes and shoes, and spread the calico out flat on the *kang*. He held the warmed wine in both hands and painstakingly washed her body. To him, she was the cleanest in the world. She should go clean to that purest and cleanest of places.

Although he hadn't touched a drop of the wine he felt slightly dizzy while he was binding her in the calico. His vision and his thoughts seemed entirely unconnected. He kept thinking of the two of them in the willow grove by the river at Duangou. The moonlight would slip through the branches and weave a network of light and darkness on her face. She was so close to him. He could smell the warm odor of her body...

A man burst through the cellar door as though it had been smashed, bringing a rush of wind with him. Although this man had come on horseback, there had been no sound of horses' hooves. The intruder was holding a weapon in both hands and there was a sound of leather straps rubbing. He didn't turn his head but continued to bind her. He could sense, however, that the man had walked up to the fire and was standing there with his gun pointed at his head.

From the sound of the intruder's breathing he could tell that it was Fugeng. Fugeng had contracted asthma when he was at the mine and now always breathed very hoarsely.

He said, "I knew you were here. You even want a corpse, you cur."

He didn't turn his head but continued to bind. His iron-like back was crawling with beads of sweat and tongues of flame whipped up by the wind danced across them.

"Are you surprised that I've come back?..."

"I was expecting it."

"I've come to return something. Some things you gave Dazhenzi. I'm giving them back to you. Let's leave it at that." He threw across a parcel. It hit him in the back and landed at his feet. One of the things was the bracelet Fugeng had never let her wear. The bastard!

"We should finish off our business. Pick up your weapon."

He didn't turn his head but engrossed himself in his binding. He heard Fugeng pulling back the bolt of his rifle.

"Why don't you damn well pick up your weapon? Is it so people can say I hit an unarmed man?"

"Can you wait until I've finished binding her? I haven't brought a weapon."

"I don't have time to wait for you to attend to a woman!"

"You damn well didn't understand this woman. She didn't laugh with you, she laughed with me. She never said one sincere word to you but she told me everything."

These words obviously angered Fugeng. He hadn't turned his head and so he couldn't tell what Fugeng's face was like. But he heard him walk by from the fire and place the end of the barrel of the gun against his sweat-soaked back.

"Try to understand." Fugeng's voice trembled slightly. Then he said even more hoarsely, "You've utterly ruined my life! The things you've done and said have destroyed me! Just wait a while and I'll tell all the people of Duangou just what's really going on! I don't want gold! If you had all the gold in the world I still wouldn't want it!"

"Then pull the trigger. Aim just to the right of my ribs."

Fugeng did not fire. He stepped back, treading on the fire.

It was so stiflingly hot in the cellar that all the walls were dripping with water and the sound echoed everywhere. He still hadn't turned his head to have a look and he continued to bind Dazhenzi's body. He thought he should leave her face exposed. Her face was like the moonlight from heaven.

"Turn your face! I'll strike you yet, you cur!" Fugeng cried.

"If you don't strike me now, you'll regret it."

The gun went off. He fell to the ground as though he had been pushed. The bullet passed through his left shoulder blade and blood gushed out from the hole in front.

It did not kill him. He got to his feet and staggered towards the cellar door. He pulled the door open and fell outside amongst the weeds. He saw Fugeng stick the rifle under his saddle, mount his horse and follow the cobbled road westward along the river.

"Fugeng—" He struggled to his feet and yelled, "If you were a real man, Fugeng, you would have given me another bullet!"

Fugeng didn't turn back.

He called out once more.

Then he fell heavily to the ground.

The Earthenware Pot
Translated by J. Gondwe

At the beginning of the fourth month of the lunar calendar the river was still thickly frozen over. The wind blew smoke everywhere, and sleighs still flew across the ice, and the galloping iron-shod hooves sprayed out ice fragments which fluttered in the air like a host of demons in the feeble sunlight.

When the sleighs had passed, the river quietened into a dreamlike slumber. Not even the sound of the rending, cracking ice could be heard. In the silence, there was an air of expectation.

It had been like this for a couple of weeks, causing people to feel anxious and disquieted. The silence was disturbed only by a distant beating, metallic sound coming from behind the mountain. It was the sound of melting snow, and its muffled echo filled the dense cold air. White fog, which drifted from the thick, birch forest, enshrouded the mountain peak giving it a mysterious, mystical look. There was an astringent, almost medical smell about the fog as, quivering and rippling, it filled and then flowed over the gorge. The whole of Heilong River was enveloped by a mysterious, fearsome atmosphere.

Although the river was still frozen, spring water from further upstream had flowed down. In the end something had to happen. All the old people observed, "This hasn't happened for thirty years."

The trees on the banks hadn't yet sprouted forth green growth and worms still slept in the earth.

"Have the lower reaches of the Huma River thawed yet?" they asked. "We damn well don't want the upper reaches to thaw first!"

One night, suddenly, thunder woke the people from their sleep. The sky at night had an eerie feeling about it. By nine thirty it was still not dark and the clouds on the surface of the river were red like charcoal fires. There were many terns in the air, but it was impossible to tell where they had come from. They swirled like thick smoke above the surface of the river, screaming madly, filling the air with their cries.

The thunder was coming from within the river. The ground vibrated and the timber houses shook. People's hearts swelled and sank, their mouths dry with fear and their legs turned to jelly.

Muffled rumbles and booms caused the houses to shudder as if they were breaking. Every log creaked, grated and groaned. Dogs barked, chickens clucked, sheep bleated, horses neighed and everything was in an uproar as all-pervading as a torrential rainstorm. Things collapsed and things were shattered. Tools lying next to the *kang* were also broken.

In a split second the thickly frozen river burst taking everybody by surprise. The water flowed down from the mountain, pushing the ice before it, forming wall after wall. These walls of ice were like bulldozers, pushing the water over the banks of the river, flooding the meadows, rising up the mountain ridge and surging into the gorge.

Every birch and oak forest was washed clean away; every wooden fence, every house and all the villages were swept away by the moving walls of ice and water. The roar of the floods and the explosive sound of colliding ice walls filled the air. People, dogs, chickens, sheep and horses looked like *zhelin* fish, stunned by the bursting river; one moment pushed up by ice floes and the next swallowed up by the water.

By the time day broke, everything had settled, but the flood had not receded. The ice floes charged about in the water like wild horses, splashing spray up ten yards high. Flock after flock of terns screamed and chased *zhelin* fish that had been tossed up by the waves.

People from the four villages of Yunshan Gully had fled, almost empty handed, to the mixed forest on the top of Huode Mountain. The mountain, formed long ago by lava, was reddish brown and half barren. In the tangled, mottled gorge at the foot of the mountain, the walls of ice had created a tranquil lake. Dead fish floated on the surface like a thick layer of oil. Terns swooped and soared in front of the villagers' eyes, while the drops of water from the terns' wings sprinkled on their faces like rain. The villagers stared blankly at the birds, the fish and the water with their faces like iron, their eyes dull as if they were still dreaming.

All they owned had been flung over into the gully near the ice wall. Their hearts were as numb and cold as the slush underfoot. They watched as a dog slid off an ice floe, a horse was swallowed by the waves, and cupboards, tables, clothing and household articles floated in the water. Nobody moved; it was as if these weren't really their possessions.

"Hey, what about Zhao Laozi?" someone cried.

Nobody knew who had cried out, but it disturbed everyone like a rifle shot, confusing them all, causing as much commotion as if someone had just been shot. Confusion reigned for a while, but then the villagers became dazed again; adults drew their children tightly to them and small mouths grimaced in pain. Nobody dared cry out, except a few strong young men who shouted a few words, and, under the gaze of almost a hundred pairs of eyes, then ran along the bare mountain ridge out of the forest.

"That old bugger!" The men cursed as they ran. "This is the end of the road for him. He wore his wife to death and wore his son and his daughter-in-law to death. Now it's his turn."

It was as if they didn't want any emotion to tear at their heart strings. When the men were out of sight, a few elderly villagers heaved a sigh, and slowly spat out some words. "He was seventy-three."

"He is one year older than me, seventy-five. He moved to One Finger Gully the year his woman died. He was the best at Pantou Goldmine."

"In the winter *Enqing* festival and in the spring *Lamaosha* you never saw him rest. It was all for that woman."

"Woman? I think it was more for the gold. I heard that he had this much—"

One of them gesticulated, and several cavernous mouths gaped wide. For a long time the only sound to be heard was their breathing.

"He was extremely poor. He had been so poor that he feared poverty."

"Even when he had money he didn't know how to spend it. Otherwise he wouldn't have waited until he was sixty to find a woman who was being married for the fourth time. It's not certain whose son that was, either."

"That woman was really very beautiful when she first arrived at Pantou Goldmine. She was so fair and her flesh so plump that you couldn't feel her bones."

"It's no wonder. That Laozi took what he could get and really went for it."

At this point, several elderly women stiffened their necks. Their faces became as cold as iron again and they cursed vehemently, "Men! They are always bastards!"

The sun had not yet risen when the few young men who had run off, covered in mud, headed for One Finger Gully. They were like wounded muntjac, standing with dazed eyes on the narrow path at the mouth of the gully.

Though wild draught animals had used that narrow path, Zhao Laozi was probably the only person to have done so. In the gully, apart from some hardy willows and stunted bushes, there was not a patch of ground that could even yield a potato. Zhao Laozi moved here alone, and built a Russian style *mukeleng*. It was said that he buried his wife underneath the floor. His son, daughter-in-law and unborn grandson had died even earlier. During the plague they collapsed together on a boat, before it had time to dock at the Huma River wharf. From that time on, he was seldom seen, except when he came to the mountain in winter, to hunt deer.

The men stood at the mouth of the gully, looking steadily downwards. The gully was completely filled with water. Ice floes rose high on the crest of waves and bumped against precipices, sending up quaking shudders that seemed to shake the clouds. One of them said, "The old bugger probably drowned long ago."

The men's faces glistened in the cold air as they gritted their teeth and swore. They lit cigarettes and smoked as they watched the terns screaming and wheeling, turning and swooping.

The young men seemed to be paralyzed, unable to think.

Nevertheless, they still felt that something was wrong for Zhao Laozi to just disappear without sight or sound. Zhao Laozi didn't have a proper name; he was the first manual laborer to arrive in the region. When he was young, he was called, Zhao Laogong (Laborer Zhao); and when he grew old he was called Zhao Laozi (Master Zhao). People here said he had saved a pot of gold, so that he could marry that woman. Young people didn't believe it and once they had asked him, but he had emphatically denied it. Still the older people firmly believed that he had a pot of gold. If he didn't, then why did he live with such zeal and vigour? That old bugger really had a taste for life. With a gleaming forehead and dancing fire in his eyes, he had something of an immortal air about him.

"Look! Zhao Laozi's house!" someone shouted suddenly and spat out his cigarette.

"Look—" he shouted again. The men rushed forward, as if catapulted, to stand under the thick plum trees that had blocked their view so they could see more clearly.

Zhao Laozi's *mukeleng* was bobbing about steadily in the water. One moment the waves pushed it to the top of the ice floe and the next submerged it. They were amazed to see that the oiled paper sealing the windows hadn't torn, and that the animal skin that had been nailed on the wall to dry was still firmly in place. And—fuck the bloody devil—even the string of hot peppers hanging from the eaves was still there.

But even more amazingly, there was Zhao Laozi, who was swimming in the water like a duck about to lay eggs.

He was wearing a black cotton padded coat and trousers. He never seemed to take them off, not even in summer. The cotton padding showing in many places had become swollen and waterlogged. Zhao Laozi sank down and then floated up in turn as he swam towards the house. They couldn't work out why he wasn't inside when the river broke. Some people said that at night time he didn't sleep inside the house, but put a lock on the door and slept in a shed he had built beside the birch grove in the high mountain pass.

He would guard the door like a bear in his den. But nobody had taken any notice of him for a long time. He had lived by himself in the gully for almost ten years.

Terns were screaming just above his head.

Zhao Laozi wasn't able to swim any more; his arms were fully extended with exhaustion. A sheet of ice bigger than a house moved across in front of him. "Does he want to die inside his house? The old bugger—is he going senile?" The men saw him try several times to clamber onto the sheet of ice. Water sprayed high in the air; after a while he lay still, floating on the water.

"Hey, Zhao Laozi!" the men shouted and cursed, but not one of them jumped down.

The wind penetrated their clothes and their teeth chattered violently, so that they couldn't clench them. They all thought that it would be better if they had a little wine to drink. Zhao Laozi caught their attention again and they swore in surprise.

"Zhao Laozi, you son of a bitch!"

To their astonishment, Zhao Laozi clambered up onto the sheet of ice. He tried to stand on it, but before he had time to secure his footing, a wave pushed another sheet of ice against it. A rumbling, muffled boom followed, and Zhao Laozi was hurled through the air like a rock. He was thrown onto the edge of the bank, and then in an instant swept back into the flood by a surge of icy water. There was no sign of him—not even his hat was still afloat.

The men bellowed in fear and surprise. Something compelled them to try to rescue Zhao Laozi, so they rushed to the bank near where he had disappeared.

They arranged to pull him out, although he weighed about three or four hundred pounds. They couldn't wring the water from his cotton padded suit. He toppled down on the spot as if he were asleep, with a serene expression on his face, moving both arms up and down as though he were clawing at water. Suddenly he sat up and regurgitated a lot of water. It was like horse urine, stinking of tobacco and wine. Zhao Laozi sneezed loudly twice and, rubbing the crown of his head, cursed the water.

"Bloody hell, it's so strong... Where's my hat?" he demanded.

The men laughed. "You were given your life and you still want your damned hat!"

"I have been rafting on the river for five years. I can't let this little bit of water swallow me. Do you have any wine?"

His dull, bloodshot gaze rolled over the group of young men surrounding him.

"You still want wine when your piss has frozen in your bladder!"

The young men all laughed in a cynical way, and continued to mock and swear at Zhao Laozi.

He sneezed again twice and, gripping a tree, he stood up shakily. He gazed far into the distance, and his eyes flashed as he stared at his house. "After a drink of wine, I couldn't care less about those sheets of ice," he muttered.

He shut his eyes, and his dry, hard, bear-leather face glowed like steel. The look of Zhao Laozi's glowing face made the young men's eyes widen. It was like seeing him again as he travelled seven hundred miles for ten pieces of gold, without stopping for breath, delivering a letter to the Black River superintendent for Master Zhang's accountant. He hadn't eaten for three days and had still run faster than a horse...

"How much gold do you have? Bloody hell, swap it for your life!" the young men sneered.

One nugget weighed just over six yuan, which was not much more than a grain of rice. In silence the young men stared at Zhao Laozi, who kept on gasping. He opened and shut his gashed and bleeding thick lips.

Suddenly Zhao Laozi opened his eyes, in which the veins were fiery and throbbing. For a moment he seemed to read the men's thoughts. Tightening the deer-sinew belt around his black padded cotton jacket he said, "Life isn't worth much. Of all the workers who came with me to the Pantou Goldmine, not one lived to fifty."

A wave broke, showering Zhao Laozi and the young men. The fire in the young men's eyes went out, but Zhao Laozi's eyes burned more and more intensely with what looked like a little spite.

"Hell. People must have dreams in order to live," said Zhao Laozi, wiping the water from his face with his purple hands and lighting a cigarette rolled by one of the men. As he inhaled deeply, his Adam's apple quivered. He let the smoke slowly stream from his nose for a long time. He said, "Don't you sons of bitches understand the meaning of life?"

Zhao Laozi slowly headed for the bottom of the gully. He was limping a little on one leg and his shoulders were swaying. However, before he could get to the water's edge, it suddenly dawned on the young men that he was getting away, so they rushed to seize him.

"You old bugger, how much gold is really in that house? Is it worth throwing away your life?" they demanded angrily.

"A whole pot full!" Zhao Laozi's eyes slashed the men's faces like two cold, glinting knives.

With a hollow laugh the young men taunted him: "Liar, are you sure you're not dreaming?"

"Dreaming...? Do you bloody well know what gold is?"

Zhao Laozi struck one of the men in the face, and then knocked another one down. His expression was fixed and he seemed suddenly to have grown. A kind of uncontrollable energy exploded out of his withered body. In the twinkling of an eye he drove several broad-shouldered, powerfully built young men back more than a yard. Without giving them a second glance he dived into the icy water and swam towards his house.

The sun rose, and the shining surface of the water was like a sheet of glass. The men stared as Zhao Laozi clambered up onto the sheet of ice.

Limping like a wounded bear, he made his way towards his timber house, less than three yards away. Suddenly he fell and rolled over a dozen times or more, eventually tumbling in through the door.

More and more terns gathered, fluttering to and fro over the water like a cloud, probably because there were so many fish trapped in the water there. The birds' screaming reverberated through the valley like muffled thunder.

The young men grew numb and cold, their faces expressionless, their whitened lips tightly closed. Waiting a long time for Zhao Laozi to emerge, they saw the terns circling the timber house, swirling about like a whirlwind.

Just then, a wind rose on the river, whipping the waves up even more. The house rocked, shuddering convulsively. The sound of colliding ice floes echoed around the valley from the forest on one cliff to the forest on the other. The startled terns, spiralling around the roof of the house, screamed horrifyingly. Suddenly the sheet of ice beneath the house split apart and the house steadily sank as water blocked the doors and windows.

The men's hearts contracted with alarm and they cried out. But then their faces lit up and they relaxed.

They saw that a window had been broken. Zhao Laozi, clasping something wrapped in a red cloth, emerged and toppled into the waves, floating on the surface of the water like a dead fish. The reflection of the red object bobbed and flashed on the surface of the water.

Behind him, the house slowly sank. A dense dark mass of terns remained on the roof but they didn't make a sound. The feathers of their fluttering wings radiated a silvery lustre in the brightening sunlight. Just as the house was about to sink completely, the terns took off and spiralled in mid air like a floating cloud, or a thick column of smoke, ascending out of sight.

Zhao Laozi slowly swam towards the bank. With one arm he tightly grasped the red object and with the other he paddled awkwardly. Waves pushed him and pulled him back and forward. One moment the ice floes pushed him down into the water; the next, they propped him up. He had just gone round one sheet of floating ice when another surged over him. The two sheets of ice collided with a resounding thud.

Before the men could shout out in horror, Zhao Laozi had disappeared without a trace. A veiling shroud of mist rose from the surface of the water and the rumbling echo which reverberated through the mountain valley chilled the hearts of all who heard it. But as the mist gradually thinned, Zhao Laozi miraculously reappeared on the surface of the water. He was still clasping the red object and still paddling steadily but awkwardly.

He was less than twenty yards from the bank when he was swept into a whirlpool. A sodden branch blocked his way, causing him to be dragged down. The whirling eddy slowly moved forward, but it was suddenly smothered by another set of large waves. By sheer good luck, Zhao Laozi found himself pushed onto the bank, safe at last.

The men rushed over. Hunching over, and embracing the object wrapped in the red cloth, Zhao Laozi stood up unsteadily. Without even glancing at the young men he made his way forward, stumbling and falling. Rocks brought to life by his stumbling feet rolled noisily down the mountain slope and plopped into the water. His face was as tranquil as a spring in a meadow. The drops of water caught in the furrows of his wrinkles glistened and gleamed. His bloodshot eyes were rheumy like a drunk's, veiled by a mysterious dream-like mist.

The young men seemed to be paralyzed by Zhao Laozi's dreamy expression as they watched him walk into the distance. He walked strongly and sturdily, though still lurching and stumbling. He didn't seem to have taken any notice of them at all.

He entered an oak forest.

The young men, in a chaotic pursuit, stampeded up the mountain slope.

Without looking back, but hearing the sound of the feet behind him, Zhao Laozi began to run, winding and twisting like an unwieldy bear fleeing for its life. He made his way through the oak forest tortuously and fled to the mountain slope opposite, which was covered with wild grass and camphor trees three feet high, with small white shining leaves.

"Hey. You old bugger, let us have a look!" the young men called, shouting abuse and increasing their pace.

Zhao Laozi ran even faster. His limp became even more pronounced, as he lurched from side to side. Grass and leaves whipped against him with a swishing sound like the whetting of a knife.

Suddenly he stumbled, and then came a muffled sound: God knows where it came from. The sound sliced at the men's hearts like a knife. They came to a dead halt quite a distance away. They gazed at Zhao Laozi with utter astonishment and extreme fear. Like a vagrant spirit he slowly stood up from a large withered clump of small-leafed camphor grass that had been flattened by his fall. He was covered with grass and leaves. He headed straight in the direction of the sound.

The young men saw a stream of white hot air rising above his head. His eyes had lost their color and without the slightest flicker or sparkle they seemed to have turned to stone. The young men approached him slowly, and in terror they watched him squat in the grass hollow where the object wrapped in red cloth lay smashed open. He sat there long enough to have smoked a pipe. Reaching out with two arms like pine branches, Zhao Laozi cautiously unwrapped the red cloth. Inside were the segments of a broken black earthenware pot. Only then, the young men saw that the earthenware pot was empty. —Perhaps it always had been and the gold had only been a dream.

White steam rose in puffs above Zhao Laozi's head. His thick hard hands trembled as he reconstructed the earthenware pot, piece by piece. When completed, the pot still had its white thunder cloud pattern on the neck and lid. After that, he rewrapped the pot in the red cloth, and gathered it up. As he straightened his shoulders, he trembled all over.

He seemed to be weighing the pot in his hand as he walked off on the crisp, whitened grass.

Without a backward glance, he headed for the mountain tops. Behind him stood the stupefied young men. Behind them were the mountain, the valley, the water, the ice floes and the screaming terns.

Dog Head Gold

Translated by R. O'Hanlan-Mullar

*On the night I heard this story in Harbin, I set out on a journey. I travelled day and night, changing from train to motor car, and then from motor car to horse. It was a pity that when I reached Black Xiazi Gully at the upper reaches of the Fabielaer River, Slipped Pants Li had already died. He had been dead for three days from a disease of the joints of his bones. Slipped Pants Li was one of the first group that had been sent into Black Xiazi Gully. He was the only one who had survived. That year he was only sixteen years old. There was quite a lot of gold in Black Xiazi Gully, both mountain and sandy gold. But the water there was so incredibly poisonous that it could kill you. Even if you did manage to survive you would be next to useless. Everyone who had been there said that this was what heaven intended. Was there anyone who had ever taken gold out of this place? The Russians had been there. The Japanese had had designs on it and had even left a Toad boat (a boat for seeking gold) there. Up until now, though, no mine had been set up there and the place was neglected. The **mayazi** grass was as tall as a person. The forest was so dense that no bird was able to fly into it. The fog hung around all year long. From an aeroplane the gully looked like a deep lake. It was the only place that still had rabbits, black wolves and red crested owls that guarded the ginseng.*

    The bonfire was burning lifelessly. The wet wood hissed and smoke wafted out. Milk-like sap seeped out slowly from the face of the axe-cut wood. Its bitter smell made people itch. The fire had been lit as a good deed by Wang Jieshi, for whom it was no bother to go some distance to collect a few dried branches and strip off some birch bark. Slipped Pants Li stared silently through the blue flame on the firewood, looking at the rippling muscles of Wang Jieshi's back. Slipped Pants Li was scared of Wang Jieshi's wolf-like eyes. The guy was capable of anything. When Old Candlehead was leaving, he said in front of everybody that he would give Sun Hanba a piece of roe deer skin, because Sun Hanba had been sleeping on damp ground for a long time and was covered with scabies. At night when he scratched them he would make everybody else itch terribly as well. But the piece of roe skin had stayed underneath Wang Jieshi's backside because he said he was afraid his piles might play up.

Slipped Pants Li stopped, loosened the waistband of his trousers and shifted to face away from the bonfire. He pulled at a few handfuls of grass, twisted them and spread them on the stone he was using as a pillow. He had not stood up to look at the gully for three days. Whenever he moved to turn away, he got a stifling feeling in his chest and had difficulty breathing. If it were not for Old Candlehead's parting instructions to look after the kid, then Wang Jieshi could have been ordering him about like a dog, to do things—like cut the firewood. He could never outperform those guys with their bear-like strength. Wang Jieshi's face glowed like a young boy's, but the others, even Old Candlehead, said he was over forty years old.

The first time that pair of wolf-like eyes had seen Slipped Pants Li, the boy had been held by the fixed stare. There was a fire in those eyes that could have burned him up in a second. Slipped Pants Li would often wake up scared and crying during the night. If it wasn't for the vast expanse of darkness that scared him even more, and if it wasn't for the fact that he had no place to go, he would have rolled up his bedding and run away. That was last year when he was only fifteen years old. His dad had died in Dish Head Goldmine and Old Candlehead had brought him here.

"Seeing you've bloody well grown up as good looking as this, your mother must have been really pretty." As soon as he had got under his quilt, Wang Jieshi had grabbed him. His eyes had burnt blue and he had snorted with laughter. He had pushed away from him and pulled up his trousers saying, "Don't you mention my mother!" Wang Jieshi had grabbed him again and held him even tighter. He had run his other hand roughly over the boy's face and body, sniggering. "I have never been with a woman. Feeling you up is just as good as feeling up your mother!" Then he had dragged him into an embrace against his chest and Slipped Pants Li bit him on the shoulder.

From then on, whenever he saw Wang Jieshi it was like being haunted. But Wang Jieshi would not leave him alone. He would scold him, touch him, kick him, pinch his ear and flick his earlobe. It seemed that only when he mistreated him would his huge rock-like face break into a smile.

The pot that hung over the fire started making noises. The aroma of dog meat wafted out and stirred Slipped Pants Li's stomach. His whole body throbbed with pain. Everyone scuffled to sit down where the draughts of air were coming from near the bonfire. Without breathing through their noses, they stretched open their mouths and swallowed them down by the mouthful as their throats rumbled up and down. Slipped Pants Li was swallowing his own saliva as well, and with every mouthful he swallowed, his stomach felt fiery hot. Only Wang Jieshi was left lying there resting his head on his arm. He faced the wide and empty sky, and chomped his teeth together.

As there was not much salt, only a pinch had been put into the large pot. If another pinch had been added, the flavour of the dog meat would have been much stronger and it would have been even harder for the men to cope with. There was still a pinch left in the deer skin pockets of the oil cloth sacks for the next couple of days. If Old Candlehead still had not returned by the morning of the fourth day then they would have to think of something else.

They had eaten nothing for nine days now. Two of them had been poisoned from eating either wild plants or mushrooms, they did not know which. As they were dying, their faces had swollen up, ghostly white. They had groaned in agony all through the night, ripping the cotton and flesh below their stomachs to shreds. They were buried under the yellow pineapple tree that had been struck by lightning. In fact, even Wang Jieshi had no more strength to dig graves for them, so they had just piled a heap of stones onto their bodies. Slipped Pants Li did not dare close his eyes at night because he could always hear the two men crying out from beneath the tree and stretching their bloodied hands up out through the cracks between the stones.

"Will you let me have a mouthful of soup please? Let me have one mouthful of soup, I beg of you!"

Sun Hanba was the oldest of the seven people present. He stood up slowly, holding an exceedingly dented copper bowl in his hands. He gazed nervously at every pair of wide staring eyes and walked slowly towards the hanging pot.

The men propped themselves up on their arms, and stared panic-stricken at the copper bowl as if they had been burnt. The flesh on their faces trembled weakly.

The copper bowl clanged as it hit the hanging pot. Sun Hanba ladled out the hot soup, but without waiting for him to put one mouthful of it into his mouth, Wang Jieshi charged over from the bonfire like a panther, knocking Sun Hanba over and clutching his neck in a vice-like grip.

"Ahhhhhh..." Sun Hanba was rolling around on the ground, squealing like a pig.

"Have mercy on him! It was only one mouthful of soup." They all struggled to their feet and held Wang Jieshi back.

Although Sun Hanba's eyes had nearly been squeezed out of his head, as soon as Wang Jieshi relaxed his grip he flipped over onto the ground like a fish and began searching around everywhere for his copper bowl. When he saw that all of the soup had spilt out and that he could not even find where it was, he held the bowl in his hands and started crying like a child. Everyone hung their heads as he cried, not daring to look at him. Only Wang Jieshi was still lying there unmoved; facing the sky with his head resting on his arm.

They had been stranded here for over six months now. It was seventy-two days since the Dish Head gold mine office had stopped providing for them. They had not excavated one piece of gold these six months. They had run around for a month and spent three months panning through sludge. They had gone through many pick-axes, but the pan had never seen any gold. Everyone was getting really frustrated. Maybe there was no gold in this bloody place to begin with!! It looked as if it had just been mere chance that some Oroqen marksman who had hunted three stag deer in one day had also managed to collect one or two gold nuggets.

Slipped Pants Li was so hungry that very early on he had come to terms with his fate. He had often thought of escaping deep in the night when people were asleep. But he did not know the roads, he did not have a horse and all the others who had run away had died on the road out. Old Candlehead had ridden away on their only grey horse.

Now their fate lay in Old Candlehead's hands. But who could know if he would come back? When the office had signed the contract and they had moved to this new place, even Old Candlehead had held a dream in his heart. He said if he could work a thousand nuggets out of this place, he would roll up his bedding and go back home south of the Wall. He would buy a few *mu* of land, build three houses and get a wife for his old brother. That night he drank two bottles of wine, and staggered over to Widow Wei's place. Widow Wei was the most beautiful of all the women in Dish Head Gully. Even those in the office dared not compete with Old Candlehead for her. Not only was he generous with his gold, but he had a vengeful heart. What's more they relied on his mountain climbing experience and reputation as they followed his footsteps into Blind Bear Gully, group by group. At its peak there had been over three hundred people here. Now there were only seven.

The sun was still just above the mountain when suddenly Slipped Pants Li realised he could no longer smell the aroma of the dog meat. He could not see anything at all. Everything had gone black.

They did not wait for the dog meat to cook properly before dividing it up.

They were all afraid that they would not live until the meat was well done. They felt themselves gradually becoming as thin as the spiderweb strands that hung from the branches. They thought their bodies would snap suddenly and even their souls would be lost.

The dog meat was fished out of the hanging pot, and the soup distributed first. Slipped Pants Li's nerves were calmed once he had this mouthful of soup. Everyone else steadied their spirits and stared as Wang Jieshi divided the dog meat. Wang Jieshi walked to the edge of the forest, chose a straight smooth birch tree and, following the vertical line of the tree, he split it from top to bottom. He did not cut it too deeply or too lightly, and he made it into a neat birch bark tube. Afterwards, using the knife, he wired it together, twisting tightly so that not one drop of water could leak out. He did not even take notice of the eyes gazing at him as he walked unhurriedly back to the bonfire. He quickly cut two wooden plugs with his knife with which to stop up the two ends of the birch bark tube. After this he cut the dog meat into pieces, and stuffed it into the birch bark tube bit by bit. All the dog meat was stuffed into the birch bark tube.

It was already dark, so he asked Slipped Pants Li to light up the pine lights so he could see as he squashed the dog meat into the tube with a pole. After using the wooden stoppers to plug the ends, he brought out a wooden ruler to mark out seven sections on the tube. He rolled a stick of tobacco, lit it and slowly lifting his eyes to sweep the yellowing faces all around him, he said, "You can all see clearly. This is our food for three days. Now everybody fix your eyes on one section. When you've done that, I'll saw again. And after I've finished chopping don't bloody well say—this one is thicker, this one is thinner."

Since you could not see the dog meat inside the birch tube, it would be a matter of luck. Even so, everyone took a long time to pick out their section and their eyes got really tired doing it. Wang Jieshi's face dropped and he began sawing the tube, banging it against his trousers. There was not a sound as he sawed piece after piece. Slipped Pants Li felt as if it was his body that was being sawn up.

The pine lights went out. The birch bark tube had been sawn up, and everyone had run off into the darkness nursing their own section. They had all disappeared in an instant, and gone to sleep. In that vast expanse of country, no sounds of eating could be heard, not even by a ghost.

It was quiet like this the whole night.

Day had scarcely broken when Slipped Pants Li started crying loudly. "Son of a bitch!... Which son of a bitch..." It was as if a snake had bitten him awake. Blades of dried grass stuck to the top of his head as he stood up, quite stupefied. He was crying and cursing at the same time, "Which son of a bitch would do such a ball-breaking thing? My dog meat is gone..."

Last night the lad had lain down in a bed of dried grass. He had eaten only a third of his dog meat and then, hugging the section of birch bark tube to himself, he had fallen asleep. His mind had actually been active all along. He had been lying directly opposite the yellowing leaves of the birch forest in the gully. Above the forest there was a cluster of stars that kept appearing and then disappearing. If you didn't look carefully enough, you would miss seeing them. They were like sparkling fish floating on the river. They also had a clear and melodious sound about them, like a long, fine, silver, silk thread dropping down out of the sky to brush softly across his face. It was as though he had fallen into his mother's bosom. He had woken up from this warm brightness and no matter how he tried he could not see the cluster of small swimming stars. The birch bark tube had been ripped from his chest and cast on the ground.

Everyone awoke with a start at the sound of Slipped Pants Li's crying. They were all investigating the condition of their own dog meat, so nobody moved.

"Bloody hell, my dog meat has been taken off by a wolf too! The mother-fucker!" Sun Hanba threw his empty section of birch bark tube onto the ashes of the bonfire. His eyes swept back and forth like the barrel of a rifle as he took a curved knife out of his bag. "This old guy is going to have it out with him! I'm going to have it out with him!"

Sun Hanba brandished his knife as he exhaled deeply. Wang Jieshi stood up into the light of the knife. His eyes shot out a cold, fearful light as he laughingly said, "I ate it, so what are you going to do about it? You're not bloody well fit to eat dog meat again!"

They never saw clearly how Wang Jieshi shook the knife from Sun Hanba's hand, and gave Sun Hanba a punch in the cheek which flung his body horizontally for five or six feet. The muddy water splashed up high in the grass hollow where he landed.

Slipped Pants Li, however, saw everything quite clearly, but he pulled his head in tightly and his two stick-like legs trembled.

"Little Slipped Pants Li, you son of a bitch, this bastard ate your meat too, and you haven't even got your knife out yet!" Sun Hanba spat out a mouthful of muddy water and blood, and stood up shakily in the grass hollow. His eyes bulged like eggs and he howled like an animal, rushing falteringly towards Wang Jieshi.

He was flung into the watery hollow again. Wang Jieshi went after him and grabbed Sun Hanba around the neck as though he were a chicken. Arching him right and left, he hit him roughly around the head. Slipped Pants Li watched. His knife dropped to the ground with a clang, falling away from him like courage.

"Don't fight! Don't fight!" The other men called out suddenly, but no one got up to hold Wang Jieshi back. Instead they ripped their sections of birch bark tube open and wolfed down their dog meat, chewing and swallowing noisily.

Suddenly Wang Jieshi let out a cry. He retreated with both hands clutching the crotch of his trousers. Beads of sweat dripped like water from his face. Then he fell on the bonfire and rolled around curled up like a caterpillar.

"Did he bite you?" Slipped Pants Li looked at Wang Jieshi who was covered in ash from head to toe, lying motionless with his face buried in the ash. He found a bag of red medicine Old Candlehead had left and came over. He turned the body over.

"Eat a little of this, and put some on too."

"You... Get me some water."

Slipped Pants Li saw blood in the crotch of Wang Jieshi's trousers. It was seeping out from his trousers and from between the cracks of his fingers as well.

"Go, are you waiting for me to strangle you, too?"

Slipped Pants Li looked once again at the blood on Wang Jieshi's trouser crotch and took the bowl. Following the now familiar small path, he headed towards the river at the bottom of the mountain slope. The feather willows on the banks waved about noiselessly in the light breeze. The willow leaves sifted a dazzling gold light on to the surface of the river, which darkened suddenly as a school of "willow roots" swam by. No sooner had Slipped Pants Li got close to them than all the fish swam clean away. Even if they had not swum off but had leapt into the copper bowl, he would not have been able to eat them. The established practice of the mountain was that you could not eat the meat of animals that did not have fur. He looked woodenly at the calm surface of the water thinking, maybe they weren't actually fish, it was a cloud, that's all; it was all the shadow of a cloud.

He ladled out the water and returned. The son of a bitch Wang Jieshi had stripped naked in front of everybody. He had taken that thing out and was applying ointment to it. He then wrapped it up tightly in a piece of cloth. "I'll do whatever I like with my own thing! Take a look at yourselves, you'd frighten yourselves to death, you bastards!"

Slipped Pants Li's gaze slid away and landed on Wang Jieshi's ragged bag under the tall, thin, yellow pineapple tree where he slept. He rushed over there as if he was being chased by lightning, screaming, "Oh! Oh! That's my dog meat, my dog meat!"

He had not reached the base of the tree before he was flung out into the thorns by a powerful force.

He lay on the ground looking at his assailant's smooth, slippery body. He watched the latter soundlessly stuffing the dog meat into his mouth, as if it were being stuffed into a hole.

Slipped Pants Li rushed at the smooth, slippery body again. Letting out a noise like a dry tree branch, the fellow held both his arms captive with one hand while using the other hand to weigh up what was left of the dog meat. He raised his arm and suddenly tossed the meat onto the yellow pineapple tree.

As soon as the dog meat landed on the branch, it changed into a black bird. No matter how hard Slipped Pants Li shook the tree or threw stones at it, it would not come down. He saw the entire body of the black bird glimmering in a dark blue light under the white sun. Its wings flashed as they flapped back and forth and its feathers made a pleasing sound. The two devilish eyes looked like the stars he had seen at night...

On the morning of the fourth day they were all still lying there like that.

The mountains surrounding the gorge suddenly seemed to have grown much higher. The forest seemed much more dense. The wind off Heilong River could not blow through and the whole of Blind Bear Gully felt as if it was decaying. The grass had withered into balls, and the leaves had started to turn white. The mosquitoes died in droves on the piles of leaves, making the dried blades of grass turn black. The water in the pocket had gone rusty and the bubbles gave off an unbearable stench as they popped.

Slipped Pants Li shook the blades of grass from his head and glared at the black bird on the yellow pineapple tree. Its wings still glowed with the same dark light. But it was so far from him it might have been in the sky. He looked at the desolate scene as the men lay around him. When they had come into the gully, these old fellows had burned incense to the mountain god and sworn to heaven they would look after each other. Now everyone cared only about himself. Their faces were dried up and stiff like the mouldy leaves of an oak tree. There was a horrible stench emanating from their bodies. He could also smell the stench of his own body. He felt as though he were dying. Although he did not know what death was, he thought it was something that your own body gave birth to. Like the itchiness and numbness of an insect bite. Or like a hole in the body where the blood could ooze out until there was none left.

He wanted to laugh. He felt he should smile at the devilish bird before closing his eyes. He made the effort to grin but did not know whether the black bird had seen him or not, and his eyes closed slowly. The last thing he saw was the black bird shrinking. A bizarre sound came from its wings as it rode up on a puff of shining gold wind. Bubbles came out of its mouth, like a fish. The transparent multicoloured bubbles surrounded it one by one. Suddenly everything went white in front of his eyes and he could not see a thing. He felt only a burning sensation like fire on his body.

When the fiery feeling had dissipated, through his drowsiness Slipped

Pants Li heard someone singing opera. The low pitch of the Liuqin melody was bleak and graceful, but also as grating as an oil saw felling timber:

> Remember those days when with one spear and one horse I could pacify Gua Zhou. Armor of iron, spears of metal, and the blood of a man; a coat of marten, cords of silk and the wine of heroes; even without titles it was romantic. My two greying temples did not know fear.

He did not need to look to know that it was Guan from Shandong who was singing. Two nights ago the man had been affected by an unbearable melancholy and wailed the whole night through. The old scoundrel had thrown all the money he earned to the women of Yanqiuli brothel at Black River. After he turned fifty, he said that any extra year would be a bonus. He was not afraid of dying, just afraid of not having any wine. They always ran out of wine before running out of grain here. He was the first one to have fallen over, and he had not got up again since that day.

The Liuqin melody cut off suddenly. As if a wolf had bitten him on the backside, Sun Hanba cried out, "He's going! Shandong Guan is going—"

He yelled for a long time, but not one man moved. Perhaps they were unable to move. A layer of icy goose bumps rose all over Slipped Pants Li's body. His blood felt like an insect crawling limply back and forth across his skin.

"Wang Jieshi, I beg you, give him a mouthful of water." Sun Hanba gave an earpiercing wail, as though it had drifted down out of space into a grass clump, and had left only the sound of the splintered grass blades knocking together.

Slipped Pants Li saw Wang Jieshi stand up beneath the yellow pineapple tree. Half dead, he leaned against the tree trunk. He did not even look at Sun Hanba and Shandong Guan, and seemed to say into the rapidly cooling wind, "I can smell the odor of fish from the river. The weather is going to change."

"Wang Jieshi, Shandong Guan is going..."

"What are you carrying on for?" Wang Jieshi's charcoal fire eyes burned into Sun Hanba, "Whether he dies or not means less than a fart to me! If that son of a bitch Old Candlehead still hasn't come back tonight, I'm going to go and dig for mountain gold at the mine myself." Suddenly he laughed coldly. The sound of his laughter was like a big wind filling the mountain gorge. It made Slipped Pants Li feel tense from head to toe. He was so taut that he felt weightless. Scared that he would float up like a withered leaf, he dug both hands into the ground.

"I don't want to die with you, and rot in this place. There's someone who misses me. The girl of the Gao family in Dalalatai is waiting for me still!"

Before Wang Jieshi finished speaking, Sun Hanba started howling too, "I've got a wife and children in my home town too. I also have an old father turning eighty. When I came here my young son couldn't even call me daddy...!" Slipped Pants Li's skin broke out in goose bumps again, itchy this time as well as cold. Perhaps Sun Hanba really was crying, but Slipped Pants Li could not figure out why.

"You just wait for them to come and burn paper money to you."

Wang Jieshi turned over again. He always lay there so peacefully, without moving in the slightest. This son of a bitch was able to save energy. But he still had half a tube of dog meat, Slipped Pants Li said to himself. That son of a bitch has a heart as black as black. But your fate was decided by the heavens, and you could not say for sure who was going to die first.

No-one spoke that day. Everyone was waiting quietly to die, and hoping that everybody else would die before they did. They were thinking of the few things they had done to accumulate merit. Maybe these few good deeds would help them now. Neither Slipped Pants Li nor Wang Jieshi thought about anything. They had gone to sleep embracing a wind which grew cooler with each gust.

The weather changed during the night. The wind brought damp air with it. The tips of the trees had just been suffused with white, when the rain came down, followed closely by sand-like snowflakes that hit their faces like burning needle pricks. Before long, the wind had stopped and the snow came down steadily to cover the mountain in white.

Although Slipped Pants Li was buried in snow, he gradually felt his body grow warm all over. He endeavored to open his eyes to look at the fire. The fire was near where they had cooked the dog meat. The golden flames leapt over the firewood. Sometimes the flames stretched out like arms to stroke Slipped Pants Li's face lightly. Sometimes the flames left the pile of firewood like spirits and floated up to hang in mid air. All the people Slipped Pants Li knew well were in the flames: his dad, his mum, and the girl he had grown up with. Old Candlehead was there, too. As long as the fire did not go out they would not leave him.

"You fucking cunts, do I still have to wait on you sons of bitches?"

Slipped Pants Li was woken by Wang Jieshi's cursing. He suddenly came out of the illusion of the fire to realize he was buried quite deeply in the snow, and the cold had penetrated right into his bone marrow. He struggled for quite a while and leaned forwards in the snow. He heard Wang Jieshi repeatedly cursing "Fucking cunts" and saw him covering the newly cut birchwood poles of the horse stalls with grass.

The horse stalls were completely covered by the fine light dawned. Wang Jieshi carried those who had been buried in the snow one by one into the horse shed. He carried each one and cursed each one thoroughly, until he got to cursing Old Candlehead. Everyone understood why; this fall of snow had sealed off the mountain for them. Old Candlehead would not be able to come in and they could not get out.

White steam came off Wang Jieshi's head and neck like a food steamer from carrying those corpse-like fellows into the horse shed. He gulped air with difficulty. His eyes stared straight ahead. He fell over many times in the snow, only just managing to get up again.

"I'm carrying you for your mother's sake." Wang Jieshi was like a black bear as he threw him into the shed onto the grass. He bent down to take Slipped Pants Li's chin between his fingers and say, "You son of a bitch, let me be your step-father, hey?"

Slipped Pants Li pulled back from Wang Jieshi's hand and turned his head away.

"Hey, you son of a bitch, you're still not pleased about the idea of your mother and me, are you? If your mother had been with me, you would have lived in ease and comfort too. Your step-father has lots of money!"

Wang Jieshi laughed wickedly. Before retreating from the shed he kicked Slipped Pants Li resolutely and gave his neck a good wrench.

He gathered the snow from around the shed and packed it down firmly, then carried in two large bags of dried grass. He kicked Sun Hanba saying, "Men, I think you should all strip off your clothes. I can't go outside and work without clothes."

"But then we'll freeze to death in here!" Sun Hanba protested, groping for the knife beneath his body.

"Put your knife away, you bastard!" Wang Jieshi stepped on the arm that grasped the knife. "Would I let you freeze to death? You vile sons of bitches. I'll cover you with grass, and you can nestle down into it and you'll be warmer than you'd be in a woman's bosom. You'll die of happiness, you bastards."

Wang Jieshi put on the various sweat-stained, fish-smelling short gowns and trousers one after the other, and went out, carrying the pick axe and spade on his shoulder.

He went to the mine, which lay in a water gully near a row of mountain millet. Just before he left, Old Candlehead had made a *Qing* (pit) here. Although no gold had been panned here, he concluded that the place would be lucky. It was because he was lucky this way that he was also able to negotiate grain, meat and wine deals with the management.

This water gully was a long way from the horse shed—further than the row of millet and the blackness of the birch forest. But Slipped Pants Li could hear the sound of the pick-axe. That fellow always worked as if he had gone insane. The tip of his pick-axe breathed fire, and steam sizzled out of the sweat he dropped on the rocks.

In fact everybody in the shed could hear the noise of Wang Jieshi's pick-axe. The sound was transmitted beneath the ground, and shook them so much that they could not shut their eyes all day. In their hearts they cursed him in rage and jealousy: "It's so bitingly cold! That son of a bitch, for the sake of a woman he doesn't even care about his own life."

By nightfall, Wang Jieshi had not come back.

That night the men in the shed were so cold they could hardly stand it. Sun Hanba took out his fire axe and fire stone to set the grass alight. Everyone rushed over to stop him. They fought non-stop until nearly daybreak before finally settling down. It was a good thing there had been this battle and they had been able to work up a sweat. Otherwise, even their brains would have frozen into icy jelly.

Wang Jieshi returned at daybreak the next day.

Lumps of blood and ice had congealed all over his face and body. His hands were wrapped around a stone as big as a dog head. He tumbled over as he staggered to the door of the shed and the rock rolled off a long way.

"My little woman! Little woman—" he howled hoarsely. He crawled over like a black bear to hug the rock to his chest again. He stood up slowly, staring straight ahead, gazing at the men inside the shed. The teeth of the grinning mouth were quite wet with blood and he laughed: "Let me dig! Look, all of you! Look, you sons of bitches, dog head gold! You could get at least three to four pounds out of this!..."

Slipped Pants Li was stupefied. He saw clearly that it was only a stone!

"How come you're not bloody well laughing? You sons of bitches—" Wang Jieshi pulled one birch wood pole from the horse shed and leaned on it as he left the shed and walked towards the snowy road that headed out of the gully.

He was a long way away, but Slipped Pants Li could still hear Wang Jieshi laughing and cursing, "You sons of bitches..."

Slipped Pants Li felt as though his heart had been ripped to pieces and scattered like snowflakes in the mountain gorge by the wind that tore into the shed.

The fire axe cracked against the fire stone a few times. Sun Hanba called out like a ghost and laughed loudly. He set the grass alight. The flames leapt up high to make a hole in the horse shed. Slipped Pants Li looked in terror at the golden glow of the flames that were dancing and floating about like demons. The ash flew up from the fire, like innumerable black birds dashing into the sky. The black birds took everything from his heart, and he followed it, flying with it into the iron-like sky.

The Clock
Translated by E. Cole

I do not believe this is a true story. Neither is this type of legendexclusive to the Wulubayajier tribe of the Oroqen from the Daxing'an Plateau, but it is also to be found far away in Europe in the Aegean culture of Mt Ido on Crete.

He escaped. The fog struck his face like rolling waves of water, one after another. Even if he had opened his eyes wider, he would not have been able to see anything at all, and he relied entirely on memory in finding the horse yard. When Mother let go of his hand, she had pressed something to his breast. It was possibly some iodine or perhaps some bear fat balm. But after fleeing down the slope of the river bank he was unable to find it. The grass there was so high it was impossible to see the ground.

The wind was cold, the fog damp. His wounds began to smart as if salt had been rubbed on them. On the previous afternoon his father had hung him from a hitching post and thrashed him until the whip frayed. He kept at it as if he wanted to kill his son in one breath. But the boy had grown up to inherit his father's backbone. He endured the whole thing and didn't utter a sound.

The Shaman had said that he was possessed, that the shadows and forms of ghosts and demons surrounded and engulfed him. He said he could see all this even before he entered the family's tent, the *zuoluozi*. His mother could only weep. She could not bear to watch Father take off his deer-skin coat and whip their son. She hid inside the *zuoluozi* and pierced the palm of her hand with a knife, watching the blood flow from the wound. Every household and family in the village burned incense and said prayers amid the sound of the Shaman's drums and bells. Old women knelt before the fire and chanted, "Helele! Bless us, O Huriye."

The villagers had caught next to nothing in the hunt all winter, but he didn't understand why he should take the blame for this catastrophe. His father had made him understand. His father had found out just the day before that he was intimate with Baidanjiya of Aokete. Using the whip he told him, "If you are my son, go and die in that widowed bitch's *zuoluozi.*" His father told him that Baidanjiya's mother was cursed, that she was unclean. She had jinxed her husband's parents and then placed such a curse on the man until he died. Baidanjiya had been born after his death. She was as white as milk and had blue eyes; she was not of Aokete. Wherever she and her mother walked, the fires died; wherever they settled, birds and beasts fled. They should be burned to death by heavenly fire. Otherwise we will never be able to live prosperous lives.

"You bastard. How else could you have been so bewitched by Baidanjiya? Your eyes are in your crotch, and you still have the hide to be a Wulileng marksman! You've brought even me down—why else haven't I been able to kill even one bear or catch one purple marten all winter? Your mother and all the other Wulileng women have been unable to conceive; even the sacrificial *kawawa* grass has lost its fragrance!" Finally he tired of hitting and cursing. He dropped to the ground and threw the knife down at his feet, saying, "If you don't die in that widowed bitch's *zuoluozi*, don't ever let me see you again."

Actually, his father didn't believe in the Shaman that much, but he found the shame of not catching a single bear or a purple marten all winter unendurable. His mother cut the rope with which her son was suspended and buried his head in her bosom and said, "Run away quickly, Molitu! Your father really wants to kill you. He's already sharpened the knife. When day breaks he wants your blood as a sacrifice to Bainaqia in front of all the Wulileng people."

Could it be that like his father, Bainaqia the Mountain god would gag his mouth and pay no heed to his explanations? He wanted to tell Bainaqia and all the Wulileng people that Baidanjiya was the most beautiful girl he had ever seen. She was the loveliest doe on Mt Taerdaqi. His father had said a whole lot of things about her but he had never seen her. In fact, all of the Wulileng tribe had said similar things without having seen the girl. Her mother had always been an invalid and Baidanjiya looked after her and stayed by her side all day. Only at night would she go out. So it was that they had met at night. The night pulls everything in close; the stars and moon were captured within their very breasts. But where was Bainaqia?

Molitu was running, and all the wounds on his body were bleeding. His feet crunched on the little dappled path and splashed through the watery fields. He had been running for an age but still had not emerged from the darkness. It was so dark he couldn't tell where the valley began and ended. He passed through a stretch of wood blown over by the wind, a camphor pine forest, and then descended the ridge. After just a few steps he tumbled headlong into a pitch black clump of trees at the fork of the river.

On the mountain top, a layer of thick red haze emerged above the trees. Molitu was roused suddenly by the call of a white-browed owl in a clump of camphor pines. It sounded as though it was calling out to something. Baidanjiya had said she liked this bird and that hearing it made her think of things far away. But she had never seen one. Molitu had seen the bird and it looked quite frightening. But he had heard old people say that the owl's call means the forest is empty—just like his mind was now. He had nothing to wait for, nothing to hope for. Like a leaf falling to the ground, his heart was weightless and empty. While he had been running it had seemed as if his heart had been weighed down by a rock, and step by step he had fallen into darkness.

He heard the sound of the wind in the forest and the water flowing in the river, and he could smell the delicate fragrance that wafted from the yellowing grass. He walked along the river towards Aokete and that familiar white log house closely encircled by a plank fence.

He could think of nothing now; he just kept on walking forward. His mother had urged him to do this, to go out and try his luck. Where was he running to? He shook his head. He had reached twenty-four and had never left Taerdaqi Valley; he had never even contemplated leaving it. He remembered that a few years previously he had seen a group of people from beyond the mountains with packs on their backs and red and white poles across their shoulders. They were carrying many things that looked like the animate household objects known to these people as instruments. They had no guns, horses or dogs. "This isn't their forest!" Father said as he loaded a bullet into the *bieladanke* rifle. He bent down in a clump of grass and quietly took aim at the group of people. He was gritting his teeth so much that his gums showed. "Those sons of bitches, if they fell a tree within my rifle sights, I'll drop them on the spot. A life for a life. Do you hear, boy? No matter how much money they're willing to pay, you'd better not be their guide! Those people are different!"

His father's words were full of bitterness and aggression. When the group of people vanished from his sight his father actually managed to sleep and started to snore deeply. But Molitu felt desolate at heart. He felt that the mountains had shrunk. It seemed that they and the sun were somehow missing something. He felt that he too was lacking something.

The white-browed owl started to call out once more. This bird watched over the moon for the mountain folk. He wondered what the mountain was like when there was no moon. What if there was no bird? His thoughts wandered, and his heart—which seemed to have a piece missing—was plunged into uncertainty.

He approached the tightly shut gate of the plank fence, unsure whether to call out to Baidanjiya. Just as his hand touched the gate, it opened and Baidanjiya emerged before him as if she had sprung from the ground.

"Have you escaped?" she asked.

"You must escape with me!" he said urgently.

Baidanjiya buried her head in his chest and began to sob. The sound was like that of a fawn and struck his chest like a series of blows.

"Molitu, leave and take Baidanjiya with you. She is carrying your lamb within her."

Baidanjiya's mother spoke from inside the house. This lonely, long-suffering woman began to shout as if she would split the *zuoluozi* apart: "May he be born of Molitu. He is the heir of Aokete! Now Aokete will have descendants! Ah, may the heavens protect you."

Molitu started to tremble all over and placed his hands on Baidanjiya's shaking shoulders. "Is it true—my baby?"

"He's not! He's not yours, get out!"

Baidanjiya pushed him violently and turned and ran towards the dwelling. With a bang, the door was shut and locked from the inside. Baidanjiya had been shut out.

Her mother called from behind the closed door, "Go, child! Don't worry about me, just go. Let the seeds of Aokete sprout up wherever they go!"

Molitu could tell from her voice that she wasn't going to open the door, regardless of how bitterly Baidanjiya was crying. Women of Aokete never change their minds.

Molitu suddenly felt a surge of strength and resolve. He picked up Baidanjiya and with wide trembling strides walked out past the fence.

The fog in the valley receded like flowing water. The damp birch forest covering the hill looked as though it were waiting for something. Molitu's leather boots slipped on the grass. At his breast, Baidanjiya suddenly stuck out her hand and seized his ear, saying, "Listen, the white-browed owl is calling again."

"Where? Where?" Molitu turned around but still couldn't hear the bird.

"In my belly, silly! Two little legs calling kick by kick. They're calling you!"

Molitu's face reddened and he grimaced. He gripped Baidanjiya as tightly as he could under his arm, all the while running towards the forest. The branches pulled like hands at his clothing and beat against his face. His heart felt limp and overwhelmed, but he liked running in the forest like this. The grass, the stones, the trees and the wind were all young like him, and brimming with energy.

He found an open area and put Baidanjiya down. He knelt down in front of her and placed his ear close against her belly.

"Can you hear it?" she asked him.

"Don't speak."

It was wonderfully quiet, so quiet that they could hear their two hearts trembling in tense waves. Molitu gradually began to hear something. Suddenly he began to laugh.

"Eh—it's the sound of thunder, muffled thunder!"

"It's the sound of Thunder God's drum, you silly fool!"

"Ah—" Molitu straightened and raised his hands to the sky and cried in a loud voice, "I can hear it! Boom, boom, boom!..."

This cry vibrated so forcefully that the leaves rustled and the clouds in the sky above quickly scurried away. Baidanjiya watched him; her teeth were clenched and tears coursed down her face like water.

At that very moment a gunshot rang through the forest. Molitu turned his head to look and started. They were surrounded, and leading the group was his father. Looking into the distant valley he saw that Baidanjiya's *zuoluozi* was alight. Flames rose like clouds into the air.

The cavernous blackness of the gun barrel spewed out blue smoke; but the old man's face was even darker than this blackness. Baidanjiya got up suddenly and stood between the gun and Molitu.

The gun was fired with a deafening explosion. Molitu's mother, breaking free of the crowd, fell to the earth.

"Mother!" Molitu was pulled back by Baidanjiya.

"Run, child!" came a voice from the ground.

The gun blasted again and first Baidanjiya, and then Molitu, fell to the ground. He didn't know where he was wounded. His whole body was covered in blood.

Baidanjiya stood up suddenly. Pushing Molitu away, she walked towards the gun and cried out in a loud voice, "Quickly, Molitu, run away! Run away! My horse is in the field below the ridge!"

Molitu saw clearly a cold blade glittering. His legs were struck by something heavy and he fell down; he started to crawl but fell again. He couldn't see Baidanjiya, only the flashing of the knife. At the sound of a deep and low gunshot, he jumped up and made his way, twisting and turning, through the woods and down the mountain.

He found Baidanjiya's little bay horse. The moment he swung himself onto its back, he discovered that his shoulder had been hit and that he was also wounded in his leg. He was so badly hurt that he felt as heavy as wet timber, and he couldn't even feel his foot in the stirrup.

The crowd called out and fired their guns; but they didn't pursue him. The dark mountain and the birch forest faded into the distance like a nightmare amid the sound of the horse's hooves. But the muffled sound of that thunder crossed valley after valley to follow him like the moon and the wind. There was nothing wrong with his head, yet he could distinctly hear the clear, sacred sound of drums coming from the blue-black sky.

The sound of the drums gradually faded away and he began to feel dizzy. The mountain range seemed to rush at him like a wild beast of the forest and he fell from the horse.

He awoke three days later, lying in the house of a Han Chinese. His body was covered by a floral quilt and the *kang* was very well heated. A man on the opposite *kang* was smoking. The smell of the smoke was so fragrant that it relaxed and refreshed Molitu's whole body.

"You're awake, eh? You've been sleeping for seven days." The speaker was an old man with a voice so guttural it seemed to come from inside a deep cavern, interspersed with bouts of coughing.

Molitu wanted to speak but couldn't. Through a drowsy haze he could see the old man stroking his forehead. The old man was quite thin; white, cloud-like whiskers floated to and fro before his eyes.

"There's fever in your blood. It burns in the vessels of your liver and a veritable fire rages in your lungs. You also have a chill, but if you take two more doses of this medicine, you'll be better."

The old man sat alongside the *kang* and lit a long cigarette and inhaled, neither hurriedly nor slowly. He continued to speak: "I'm looking after your horse. It's in the shed in the rear courtyard. It's wounded too..."

Molitu didn't quite hear what else the old man said. He felt as if his soul was hanging from one of the beams in the house and his mind was swinging back and forth, ready to take flight any moment. His ears were full of a humming sound. He couldn't tell whether it was the call of the white-browed owl or the sound of thunder.

He was also unsure how many days had passed. While still lying on the *kang*, Molitu opened his eyes and looked through the double-glazed window, which showed a slanting panel of featureless sky. The sky was very heavy and luminous. He could feel that it was snowing—the first snows of autumn. His senses also told him that this place was not far from Taerdaqi.

All of a sudden, an unusual sound penetrated his whole being. It seemed to bore directly into his heart—heavy, regular and distinct. "Tick-tock, tick-tock, tick-tock." His whole body unconsciously began to tremble with this sound. But what was it? It was as mysterious as the sound of the bells and drums of the Shaman's ritual dance, and as bewitching as the call of the white-browed owl or the sound of muted thunder from Baidanjiya's belly. He couldn't tell where it was coming from or how long it would last.

He sat up suddenly but was riveted to the spot as if in a trance. He saw, very close to him, a large wooden box hanging from the wall. Underneath a gleaming glass cover was a circular dish like a bronze moon. There were markings on it similar to the ones the Shaman drew on birch bark. It had two needle-like things turning on it and something that gleamed as bright as gold swinging back and forth above it. It was a living thing, the source of the sound.

"Tick-tock, tick-tock, tick-tock..."

"It's a clock. A hanging clock." It was the old man again. Pointing at the clock in its glossy black cabinet he said, "I've had it for many years. I bought it from a foreigner."

"It's alive." Molitu looked intently at the clock.

"It follows the heavenly bodies."

"Are the sun, the moon and the stars all in there?"

"No, only the time."

"Time? What's time?"

"It is night and day, sunrise and sunset..."

"Do you really need it to tell you that?" he asked, disbelievingly.

Molitu fell back on the *kang*, an icy light shining from his eyes and gave a silent curse. "Bastards, lying again!"

The old man didn't seem to mind the expression on Molitu's face. He laughed and shook his head. "How can I explain this to you? We watch it to tell the passing of days."

Do Han Chinese have to watch such a thing to tell that the day has passed? Molitu focussed his vision on the clock and listened woodenly to its resounding, regular beat. He felt as though his soul had been seized by the clock and was leaving his body.

Bastards, they're all deceitful! This living thing reared by these Han people must have a far greater use. Molitu had never believed what the Han people said. Once, when he traded his pelts, deer embryos and bear gall bladders for the Han's salt, rice, cloth and ammunition, he had experienced for himself how the peddlars with their blinking, snake-like eyes had cheated him.

He looked through the window at the crowded little town with its brick and tile houses crammed into narrow, dirty streets. The banners of inns and shop signs of every description fluttered above people's heads. At this end of the street there were several large chimneys, and the sky was stained an ashen colour from the smoke.

Night fell. He was still lying on the *kang*, unable to sleep. He was torn between despair and panic.

The clock continued to go "tick-tock, tick-tock" on the wall. The whole room resonated with the mysterious sound. The four walls cut everything else off; there was only he and this living thing in the room.

Sometimes he felt that this tick-tocking sound was forcefully yet langorously assailing him, in the same way as the clip-clop sound of the horse's hooves, the rushing water sound of the leaves, the call of the white-browed owl and the sound of thunder in Baidanjiya's belly. At other times, he felt it was like a wild beast hiding in the darkness, moving dangerously towards him, ready to pounce... Suddenly, he saw the light of the clock glimmering through the darkness. It was shining straight into his heart. He felt that it was indeed a mysterious and dangerous creature. It was undoubtedly something of great value, perhaps more precious than the sun, moon and stars—why else would the Han keep it alive?

The more the snow fell, the heavier it became, and the whiter the night became. The sound of the clock grew louder. It was like a convoy of wooden-wheeled carts coming from the valley or tree after tree being felled. He did not understand why it had so much power. It made everything in heaven and earth vibrate in time with it, and it seemed to shatter his very heart.

"Tick-tock, tick-tock." His ears were filled with this powerful sound. The wounds which covered his body began to hurt and seemed to be slowly oozing blood; his head felt as though it had been split.

This sound was too frightening. When at last he could endure it no longer he crawled off the *kang* like a frightened roe deer. He placed a wooden bracelet inlaid with gold on the table from which he had eaten, thinking it would do as payment for the food. Then he quietly left the room. When he reached the courtyard he led out his horse and fled without looking back. As he left the gate he saw the old man standing in the darkness, his eyes like torches illuminating Molitu. Neither of them said anything. It seemed there was nothing they could say.

This time as he was escaping, it was impossible for him to feel as unencumbered as when he had fled from home, for the sound of the clock constantly followed him. It seemed to surround him. It would appear in his dreams. It seemed to come from the sky and from the earth. It was his shadow; it haunted him like a ghost.

Clip-clop, clip-clop.

Tick-tock, tick-tock.

Eight months passed like this. No matter where he went, night or day, he could not get rid of the diabolical sound of that clock. He would be alone in the forest, he would wander the fields; his eyes had sunken in, his body, once of iron, was now like a dry stick, his face sallow. It seemed as if he saw nothing and thought of nothing. It was as if his life had been reduced to sitting trembling at the reins, abandoning himself to the whims of his horse's hooves, and going with the wind.

One day Molitu finally felt that he could travel no more and he returned to Mt Taerdaqi. By counting up the days, he calculated that if Baidanjiya was still at Aokete, their "thunder god" would have become incarnate. But when he arrived at Aokete, he could see neither the wooden fence nor the timber shack. The grass was long enough to choke him, there was no trace of a fire and the whole valley was so still and quiet that coming here seemed as terrifying as emerging into the world from a mother's womb.

Then, stupefied and rooted to the spot, he heard again the sound of the clock that had been haunting him all this time, the call of the white-browed owl and the sound of the thunder in Baidanjiya's belly. For the first time he sensed a tenderness in the sound of the clock.

Suddenly, he saw chimney smoke drifting out of the forest on the mountain ridge. It was rising directly into the sky to form a yellow cloud.

He climbed the hill and passed through the birch forest. When he saw a cluster of the familiar *zuoluozi*s he was dumbfounded. First, he saw two corpses hanging from a willow on the river bank. They had been bound with reeds. It was all so heartless—not even birch bark had been spared for this purpose. There was no proper frame, only a collection of birch branches that rocked and swayed in the wind. He could tell that this was Baidanjiya and her mother from the head ornaments they wore. The entrails of a variety of beasts were hanging in profusion above them as a curse. Green, glimmering blow-flies swarmed around the willow like a mist. Even from a distance, he could smell the stench of the fly-blown bodies. Then on the sands beneath the willow, he saw men humming *zheweizhehuileng* as they were skinning bears. They had evidently killed quite a few after he had left. The one his father was skinning was a huge beast, a head taller than a man; his father's head and face were spattered with blood. Women were cooking over suspended cooking pots. The green, flashing, golden sparks leapt high into the air and reddened each of the flat faces.

Those expressionless red faces filled Molitu with great despair. It was the type of despair he always felt when what he found was not what he expected. He felt that those people were very close and very familiar, but at the same time distant and strange.

The air above the river bank gradually became a universe of blow-flies. Those green, flashing metallic things were perhaps not flies at all but rather a group of spirits above the sacrificial altar, otherwise why would their buzzing sound so much like a moan? Below the green, swirling mist, the people of this cool and refreshing world began to imbibe liquor, eat meat and drink soup. Their hot and sweaty faces were still and expressionless. They clanged their wine bowls: "ding-dong, ding-dong"; they chewed their meat noisily and slurped their soup. All that energy seemed to be concentrated in their mouths. It seemed they saw nothing and thought of nothing. The entire mountain and valley were filled with the sounds coming from their mouths and throats.

These eating sounds, the ticking of the clock and the buzzing, all merged into one. Amidst this sound, all the people on the river bank looked as if they had turned to stone—only their mouths were left moving—and they gave off a green metallic glow.

Molitu sank to the ground. But even on the ground he could not find himself; he couldn't find anything. There was only a sound of chaotic shattering.

Three-Tile Temple
Translated by R. Davis

The huge snowfall still hadn't stopped when the "fireworks" began, signalling the year's end.

Nobody could remember when the snow had started falling. It snowed endlessly, as if the four seasons had blended into one. Everything was covered in snow—the valley, the forest, the road to the panning site and the wooden houses. Only the glowing of a lamp in the window gave a hint of life. The year had passed as if there had been no damned festival at all. On the 25th none of the homes had lit an ice lantern and on the 26th there were no red couplets on the trees. The 28th was the day for worship at the temple. You had to go, otherwise you would not find gold next year. Everyone had to go to worship the mountain god, but this time they could not because the sleigh that had gone to make special purchases for Spring Festival at Taan had not yet returned. Zhang Fahai had gone again with four horses and was supposed to be back on the 25th. The people of Laopizi Ravine had not slept well these past few days because of the worry. The wind made an ominous sound, and scratched like a cat at their chests.

Zhang Fahai left during the day on the 23rd. Actually, it was not his turn to go. He didn't have his own temple and he didn't need anything for the Spring Festival. He was a loner. When he first came here he was a criminal. It was said he had stabbed someone whilst stealing grain and then set the warehouse on fire. So many years had passed that no one remembered.

In early spring, when the ice melted and the spring water flowed, he panned for gold along with everyone else in Laopizi Ravine. In autumn they went up the mountain carrying guns, returning only at the end of the year. They slept on the large *kang* at the courier's place. Zhang Fahai used the leather wine-bag as a pillow. When he was awake he drank, and when he was drunk he slept. He said that this way he could cleanse his mind, and save having to think on an empty stomach, thoughts of his wife in his home county of Wendeng. He would speak about this, though he would never say what happened to her; and sometimes he would speak about his child, a girl. When he left she was six years old. Everyone guessed that, after he left, his wife had taken the child and re-married. He said life was damned well like that. After all, if he didn't think anything, he would be just a dumb animal.

That suited him, so he didn't save money. If he had any, he would eat and drink and give it away; but everybody knew that he had dreams. Sometimes when he was drinking, he would stare at a beam in the ceiling as if spellbound. His piercing gaze frightened people.

When there was snow, the sky became light early. That day, when breakfast was over, the men of the ravine went over to the accountant's office, waiting to be sent to fetch the goods for the Spring Festival.

In the centre of the room, on the waist-high Dabiela stove was a large Russian-style copper kettle which could hold a bucket of water. Steam whistled from it with a sound like a howling wolf. Everyone was sitting around the front of the *kang*, looking at Big Head He as he shaved his head. This guy had to shave his head three times a month, and it was always shiny. Big Head He used the knife blade against the direction of the hair growth. He said it was good for the natural balance of his body.

"XXXX! What's the point of staring at me!" Big Head He lifted a leg onto the table, gritting his teeth. He sharpened the blade back and forth along his trouser leg, then looked at everyone fiercely, like a hungry wolf about to gobble them up. Slowly his eyes darkened, and he said, "Someone must go to get the New Year's goods. If not, what will we take to the temple? Are we going to give the mountain god a piece of human leg meat?"

No one answered. Everyone knew that this year's blizzard had been more cruel than usual and those who had gone to make New Year's purchases couldn't make their way past the labyrinthine forest on the ridge. The wind there blew down Fabiela Gorge from Heilong River, striking the rocks with a metallic sound and cutting the lambskin coats like knives.

"Liu You should go. It's his family's turn." Big Head He lifted his leg again to use it like a strop for his shaving-knife.

"But he's sick. His hernia is giving him problems," someone answered.

"He's really picked a bloody good time to get sick. He always has hernia problems when we need him." Big Head He's eyes stared like a pair of gun barrels at the group. He looked around the *kang* for someone who would agree.

"He also has problems with his legs. Last month, when he was at Nahan chopping wood, a tree branch pierced his leg," someone from behind him added.

"Fuck him! So what are we going to do about this year's Spring Festival goods!" Big Head He was angry, his face twisted. "It's his turn. He should go, even if he dies on the way. We'll have to make him go!"

"What if I go, Big Head?" Zhang Fahai came across from the *kang* carrying the black, glossy, oily wine bag in his hand. His eyes were so narrow he might still have been asleep.

"You...you don't need to go to the temple. We don't have to use you. Liu You should go. We can't let him wreck our system. A hernia is really not a bloody disease."

"Come on, Big Head, don't push people too far." Although Zhang Fahai was calm, his eyes were wide open, and they cut back and forth across Big Head's face like a knife. "I said I'll go, and I'll go. I won't go back on my word now that I've volunteered. Why don't you send someone to get the sleigh ready?"

"All right, if you really want to go, go. I'll give you twenty pounds of pork when you get back."

"Twenty pounds? One life in exchange for twenty pounds of pork? That's not much, is it?"

"How much then? How about fifty pounds?"

"Fifty pounds... All right, you said it, Big Head. Don't bloody well take it back when the time comes."

"I'm not a man if I take it back!"

Big Head wanted to go on, but Zhang Fahai had already turned and gone. He poured a bag full of wine on the door hinge. He rubbed snow on his hands and face till they were red, slung his Russian-style rifle over his shoulder and let out a sound like a bear growling. Then he set off into the wind.

When Zhang Fahai opened the door, those inside all tucked their heads in. They slowly relaxed, heaving a deep sigh.

Whilst sprinkling his half-shaven head with hot water, Big Head He cackled strangely, saying, "I bet that bastard has done this to impress Liu You's wife!"

"That little woman can really win them over with her bright eyes, and her powder-fine face, delicate as porcelain!" When the old courier sitting on the *kang* said this, the others sniggered. As a result, the topic of conversation focussed on women's physical attributes. This was a gold panning area; most men had no wives. Once a year they took all the money they had saved and squandered it on the favors of the women in the brothel in Taan known as the White Rooms. If they didn't waste all their money in the White Rooms they would daydream about these women. Yet when they went to the White Rooms they regretted it and cursed that a year of effort was wasted on those sluts. What they really hated was the lack of women here. There were so few it was unendurable, especially over New Year. Although it seemed they were talking happily and cursing good naturedly, you could also tell from their conversation that they were sick at heart because they had left their wives and children south of the Great Wall.

Clang! No one knew who smashed the wine bowl onto the copper kettle. It crashed on the floor. There was silence. Those in the room, including Big Head He, all looked at the broken pieces of the bowl, still moving from the impact. The wind outside became more fierce, and seemed to drag their thoughts out into the snowfield, around the dark oppressive frozen pine forest, until all their remaining thoughts were torn to shreds.

The day was so cold that the mice squeaked from inside the wood pile and the walls.

Liu You leaned on the wall by the fireplace, bending and stretching one leg. His foot was still bandaged in cotton; his eyes were red and swollen. He was holding a *musedouke*, smoking one pipeful after another. His face had rusted over, losing its coppery lustre. For the last few days he sat like this, attentively listening to what was going on outside in the street. His wife sat in front of the *kang's* fireplace making the offerings to give to the mountain god. The copper kettle was filled with wine; the steamed buns had four red dots painted on them, the eggs had a round red eye on them, the dumplings had ten small folds in one side; there was also a hundred-layer cake, sticky pastry, shelled peanuts for the wine, melon seed kernels and walnuts; but there was no meat, no braised pork or pairs of smoked trotters. Today was the 28th. At noon they would have to go to the temple—they couldn't wait any longer for Zhang Fahai's sleigh. She had used dough to make the two slices of pork and a pair of trotters, added some colour, then steamed and fried them so they looked like red meat.

"No matter how good the bread substitute is, the mountain god can still tell." The woman lifted her head up from the stove. She had shadows under her eyes.

"I don't want to do it this way either. When we had a big temple, the offerings were whole pigs and sheep." Liu You's eyes were still wide, and his mouth moved as though he were chewing a buffalo sinew.

"I say we should wait longer for Zhang Fahai," his wife suggested.

"I don't want to keep hearing that."

They talked on like this—one spoke, the other answered, constantly repeating themselves.

The woman carried a bundle of sticks in from outside, put them on the edge of the *kang*, placing them one by one into the fire. Suddenly thinking of something, she said, "We should have given our gold to Zhang Fahai to take to Taan for us and to exchange for a pair of bracelets. He knows Manager Yin there."

"I know him, too. Why should we ask favors of him?" Liu You looked as if he had been stabbed in the back, his bloodshot eyes wide open.

"He does not lose out by helping us. I helped him sew a leather vest and a pair of leather socks."

"You're so damned cheap! Otherwise why would Zhang Fahai's eyes always follow you like a wolf?"

"Fahai isn't like that at all!" The woman stood up.

"As if you can damned well read his thoughts!"

"No, I can't. But I can read yours." The woman turned and walked outside the house where she mixed water into the broad beans. As she turned the millstone, soya bean curd came out from beneath it.

"Damn!" Liu You cursed, his two hands grasping his hair as if he wanted to tear it out.

"I wish I could die!" he cried out. His hernia was troubling him. It hurt so much he rolled himself up in a ball, his head resting between his legs, steam rising from his hair like a bamboo steamer.

"What did you say?" His wife ran in worriedly, her hands white from soya milk.

"This disease is going to kill me." He didn't look at her. He was concerned only with keeping a tight grip on the throbbing thing inside his crotch. It's like trying to control a wild animal.

"That disease won't kill you!"

"You're not a man," he replied as his woman sat down on the *kang* and placed her hands on his shoulder, and felt his body shaking. "If you were a man, you'd understand..."

"Haven't we got through the last two years? The mountain god will bless and protect you."

"But those people don't think like that. It's a man's world here. Gold belongs to men."

He raised his head. The veins on his neck stood out, and he howled like the "fireworks" outside.

The woman understood her man's fears but her blackened eyes filled with tears, probably because she didn't know what he had screamed about. She slowly lowered her head, her face pale and her neck straining as taut as a bow.

The man's face was like a collapsed mud wall, as he stared worriedly at the old-fashioned *Bieladanke* rifle above the window.

"I must go to Taan," he thought. After a while, he told his wife what he intended to do. "Don't be stupid." Tears ran down her face.

"With this disease, I can't touch water, nor take the cold, nor pan for gold nor stand tall—I'd be better off dead. Let them think whatever they like." He coughed a while, and covered his mouth with his hand.

Everything he spat up was red. He must have crushed something in his mouth.

"Don't be like this, Liu You! Don't! It's all my fault. I'm no good because I haven't given you a son..."

She buried her head in Liu You's back and began to sob loudly.

Liu You's whole body was shaking as if he was afraid of something. Panning gold in these cold, bleak and remote mountains, if a man did not have an iron will and an iron body then it was better for him to die. All summer he hadn't gone with the others to "La Maosha." Even when he did go to the panning site, he had to rest a few times on the way. Damn it, what meaning was there left in this kind of life? When he thought about his fears, he was most afraid of himself; it was as if at some time his spirit had been crushed. Now he lay limply on the *kang* resting silently, as though he were asleep.

The woman noticed Liu You's lips had gone white. She began to worry, shaking her man's head: "What's wrong with you? Are you all right?"

"I heard Zhang Fahai's rifle fire." He flung open his eyes, staring at the window, and said, "He can't get back through the labyrinth; the wind's too strong. I'll have to go and get him."

"You're mad!" The woman held him back. "There was no gun shot. You must be mistaken. Even if Zhang Fahai had fired his gun in the labyrinth, we would not hear it because of the wind."

"I heard a gun shot and horses neighing."

"Have a rest. You're overtired. I'll try to get our things, and we'll go up to the temple. We won't wait for him."

The woman put all the things to be taken up to the temple in a big basket. She got out her leather robe, hat and shoes and arranged them on the edge of the *kang*.

"Let's go."

"Do you think the snow would have covered our three-tile temple?"

"Even if it does, don't worry. I can remember that tree. We'll find it."

The snow kept on falling. The mountain, trees and pine cones were all under thick snow. The trees looked like furry animals in the snow as they whizzed past the sleigh. The wind blew the snow into balls. Crowds of starving birds chased the sleigh like ghosts, making strange cries. One moment the horses were deep in thick snow, the next you could see their front hooves rising out of the snow. At other times they slid on the slippery ice. It was like crossing water. One gust after another of billowing snow blew down hard on the planks of the sleigh and on the roeskin sleigh cover. Each time it sounded like a volley of exploding shots.

Zhang Fahai scooped up some snow with his hands and rubbed it over and over his face. His two leather mittens had become as hard as stone. After passing the timber depot at Crow Mountain, he could hardly move his legs. Suddenly, his earlobes became hot. He knew that this wasn't a good sign. If his legs were frozen, he was done for. His heart was beating so damned fast! He pulled down the roeskin cover and shot three times into the overcast sky. Holding the hot gun barrel, he used the gun to beat his legs through the leather cover to try to restore their movement. He did this as fiercely as if he was hitting someone else's legs. His eyes shone darkly.

"Damn!" he cursed. He did not know how long he had been beating his legs before they began to feel a little pain and slightly warm. "This is all that bastard Yin Shanming's fault. We had to find his wife just to talk over a pair of bracelets. I've wasted three days. He's probably cost me my life as well."

From Crow Mountain he headed downstream, sliding along the frozen channel used to float timber down river. It was so slippery the four horses were almost sliding completely on their hindquarters, with legs bent. Zhang used his feet to brace himself on the sleigh's runners, his two hands gripping the reins tightly. The mountain ahead of him had loomed up. Suddenly, the horizon sloped into the sky, as if the road went straight up into the air; the snowflakes were entrancing, dancing in the air like little spirits.

He caught sight of a pair of dark eyes smiling at him like springs in the moonlight rushing past him and hiding themselves in the withered pine forest. He knew those eyes. Everything she wanted to say to him was held in them. Snowflakes were sprinkled across her face, like flashes of silvery light. She had insisted he go into the forest, strip down and try on the short-sleeved leather top. She could see the scars on his chest and back. She touched the scars, each and every one. Those dark eyes were watching him through long, long lashes and tears. Neither of them said a thing; they didn't seem to need words. He followed those eyes and saw them everywhere, gleaming on each white pine leaf.

Suddenly a wolf's howl roused him from his daydream. The sleigh had entered Fabiela Gorge. The wolves, starved for a long time, came from everywhere, probably smelling the sweaty horses and the meat on the sleigh. If they hadn't been in Fabiela Gorge the horses could probably have outrun the wolves but the snow was too thick here. The horses' legs were almost completely submerged in the snow. He had confidence in his gun but there were too many wolves, at least twenty or thirty. Although he shot one after another, so that the barrel of his gun was getting white hot, the wolf pack attacked again and again, tearing the sleigh's roe-skin cover and ripping his leather overcoat to shreds. He took a piece of the meat from the sleigh and threw it down. That kept six or seven wolves occupied but the rest continued their hot pursuit. A few times they pounced and narrowly missed him. Suddenly, he turned his gun and aimed it towards the front of the sleigh. He shot the white horse in the head. Following the dull, heavy gunshot, a mark like a little red flame began burning on the white horse's head, and shot up into the sky, like a bright red cloud floating into the air. The sleigh entered the forest labyrinth, leaving the wolves behind in the gorge.

The white horse neighed as if crazed. No matter what he did, he could not hold on to the rein. When they cleared the labyrinth at the place where, on a clear day, you could see the settlement at Laopizi Ravine, the white horse fell to the ground. The other three horses and the sleigh flew over him, and glided along the slope into the huge spring they made after "La Maosha." The spring's icicles exploded as the horses crashed into it. In the midst of the collision, something hit him on his chest. Everything went dark as he lost consciousness.

Liu You insisted he would not let his wife support him, so each of them was leaning on an oak staff. They passed west of the ravine, where the ground was covered in willow catkins. They continued towards the pine forest. No one knew when the pine forest had been hit by lightning, turning it into a mass of burnt-out trees. Neither did anyone know when the trees had begun to grow again, putting out new branches, even more dense and dark than before. Although the sun had finally broken through, the snow still lay thick upon the ground and the wind wound its way through the forest. Anyone who heard the lazy sound of the wind shook from head to toe.

"The snow is so thick, I'm really afraid we won't find our little temple." Liu You's teeth chattered in time with the blasts of the wind.

"We will. I remember that tree." It was as if the woman walking at his side had found a kind of peace here. Those dark eyes of hers were so bright that you could see every dancing snowflake reflected in them.

"How come I can't remember? All the trees here look the same."

"They don't look the same. Our tree has a large branch that reaches east. I even tied a red strip of cloth on it."

"Does anybody else know where our little temple is?"

"No one. You don't know where other people's temples are, do you?"

"Some say each gold-panner has his own mountain god. Actually, I think everyone worships the same one. What do you think?"

"I don't know."

"My father said that our family's mountain god is from the Qi State."

"Big Head He says his god is from Henan."

"Probably is. When his family goes up to the temple, they must kill a chicken."

"Oh," the woman replied and walked on. She seemed to have seen something. Using her hand to shield her eyes from the glare of the snow, she stared into the depths of the forest.

"What are you looking at? Is it our tree?"

"No." The woman stopped, as if she was watching her man at a distance, and said, "I thought I saw someone walking across in front of us."

"Whom did it look like?"

"Like Zhang Fahai."

"Zhang Fahai again! I've told you before..."

"I won't listen. That evening when you hurt your leg, he brought you home on his back."

Liu You didn't make a sound—he was leaning on a tree. The light left his eyes. Only he and Zhang Fahai knew that his leg hadn't been pierced on a tree branch, but on a knife. He had gone to steal Zhang Fahai's gold and Zhang Fahai had stabbed him. Liu You didn't know why Zhang Fahai had not killed him, but only stabbed him in the leg. Here, killing a deer and a man amounted to the same thing. No one would have known. "Tell me why you planned to steal my gold?" Zhang Fahai used mercurochrome to dress the wound on Liu You's leg. Giving him a bowl of deer blood wine, he added, "Tell me the truth, I might give you the gold." Liu You told Zhang Fahai he wanted it to make a pair of bracelets for his woman. He had promised this to his wife for so many years. Now that he was sick, he would not be able to get that much gold again. "For this!" Zhang Fahai snorted, saying "You came to steal my gold because of this! You're not a man! Piss off, go on, get lost!" Liu started off. It was dark and over three miles back to the settlement. Zhang Fahai caught up with him, and without a word, he put him on his back and carried him home. From then on, Liu never knew how to take Zhang Fahai. He always felt as if Zhang Fahai had something over him: that he owed some sort of debt.

"Zhang Fahai probably has a little temple too," he suddenly said to himself, thinking out loud. Liu was always like this, thinking, pondering to himself. No one knew what he was thinking, until suddenly he would say something.

"Probably." The woman replied indifferently. She was still looking intently around the forest.

"I think that even if he doesn't have a real three-tile temple, he still has one in his heart."

"Probably."

"And I think he has a very strong grip on life. I heard those people who exiled him here say he had only a few years left. He still has a bullet in him. But look at him, he's lived many years, lived..."

Not waiting for him to finish, his wife walked off into the forest. She stood in front of a slender tree that had been burnt out by a lightning strike. This tree had only one branch reaching east. On top of this bare branch was thick snow and long icicles underneath.

The red strip of cloth was still there. His woman swept the snow away from around the tree with her hand. But no matter what she did, she couldn't find the three-tile temple. She knelt there, and scooped up some snow with her hands.

"Are you sure it's this tree?"
"Yes. I know that strip of red cloth."
"Maybe someone stole our tiles?"
"No, they couldn't have."
"Maybe the wind blew them away?"
"No, it couldn't have."
"Then you tell me. Where are they?"
"I don't know. Maybe heaven didn't mean us to find it!"

As she spoke, the woman began sobbing, taking the things one after another from the basket and putting them on the ground.

"God damn it!"

Liu You cursed and threw down the cane. He grasped the blackened tree trunk and collapsed to the ground like a pile of mud. He stared at the sky, saying "That year..."

What he wanted to say was, one night in that year when the lightning struck the pine forest, the mountain god's temple east of their village had collapsed, and was reduced to rubble. All the people of Laopizi Ravine had fearfully locked their doors, trying to work out who had offended heaven. Yet they couldn't figure it out. On the third day, the fire on the mountain went out, and everyone had gone out in the rain to slaughter a horse and two sheep. After the day of the sacrifice, each person took a few clay tiles and went home. From then on, every family set up its own temple on the mountain. But from that day on they never had any peace of mind. Was this what the mountain god intended?

"Damn! I came to burn incense and he's turned his back on me!" Suddenly Liu You felt pressure on his heart as if there was a large weight pressing down on it.

His woman stretched out her hand, touching his face. Her heart beat loudly. His face was already cold, becoming as hard as a rock.

Zhang Fahai led the two surviving horses down from the summit and back to the village. Everyone had closed their doors and gone up the mountain. On his horses' backs were the gifts the people were supposed to take up to the temples.

Congealed blood dotted one of his cheeks, its red color making his face look even more ghastly. He held the horses' reins and, passing the footprints in front of Liu You's door, nonchalantly headed off towards the mountain. On the bright ground covered by willow catkins, he and the shadows of his horses gradually faded, becoming merely three small black dots.

The "fireworks" stopped but the snow kept falling. All was quiet, as if every snowflake was in deep thought. He walked into the peaceful forest. For the first time he felt the snow was clean, the whole world was clean.

He walked up to the tree with the red cloth tied on to it. The woman kneeling on the snowy ground was already stiff, but her face was as beautiful as a peach blossom. Her dark eyes looked as if they could see into heaven.

From his bosom he got out a pair of gold bracelets and put them on her. The whole forest was filled with their dazzling golden light. The man, the tree, the sky and the snowflakes all became suffused with gold.

He stood by the woman's body for a long time, as if he too saw something in the sky. Snowflakes fell gently on his body, and, together with the two horses carrying the New Year's goods, he became motionless.

CORNELL EAST ASIA SERIES

No. 2   *China's Green Revolution*, by Benedict Stavis

No. 4   *Provincial Leadership in China: The Cultural Revolution and Its Aftermath*, by Fredrick Teiwes

No. 8   *Vocabulary and Notes to Ba Jin's Jia: An Aid for Reading the Novel*, by Cornelius C. Kubler

No. 14 *Black Crane 1: An Anthology of Korean Literature*, edited by David R. McCann

No. 15 *Song, Dance, Storytelling: Aspects of the Performing Arts in Japan*, by Frank Hoff

No. 16 *Nō as Performance: An Analysis of the Kuse Scene of Yamamba*, by Monica Bethe and Karen Brazell (videotapes available)

No. 17 *Pining Wind: A Cycle of Nō Plays*, translated by Royall Tyler

No. 18 *Granny Mountains: A Second Cycle of Nō Plays*, translated by Royall Tyler

No. 21 *Three Works by Nakano Shigeharu*, translated by Brett de Bary

No. 22 *The Tale of Nezame: Part Three of Yowa no Nezame Monogatari*, translated by Carol Hochstedler

No. 23 *Nanking Letters, 1949*, by Knight Biggerstaff

No. 25 *Four Japanese Travel Diaries of the Middle Ages*, translated by Herbert Plutschow and Hideichi Fukuda

No. 27   *The Jurchens in the Yüan and Ming*, by Morris Rossabi

No. 28   *The Griffis Collection of Japanese Books: An Annotated Bibliography*, edited by Diane E. Perushek

No. 29   *Dance in the Nō Theater*, by Monica Bethe and Karen Brazell
   Volume 1: Dance Analysis
   Volume 2: Plays and Scores
   Volume 3: Dance Patterns
   (videotapes available)

No. 30   *Irrigation Management in Japan: A Critical Review of Japanese Social Science Research*, by William W. Kelly

No. 31   *Water Control in Tokugawa Japan: Irrigation Organization in a Japanese River Basin, 1600-1870*, by William W. Kelly

No. 32   *Tone, Segment, and Syllable in Chinese: A Polydimensional Approach to Surface Phonetic Structure*, by A. Ronald Walton

No. 35   *From Politics to Lifestyles: Japan in Print, I*, edited by Frank Baldwin

No. 36   *The Diary of a Japanese Innkeeper's Daughter*, translated by Miwa Kai, edited and annotated by Robert J. Smith and Kazuko Smith

No. 37   *International Perspectives on Yanagita Kunio and Japanese Folklore Studies*, edited by J. Victor Koschmann, Ōiwa Keibō and Yamashita Shinji

No. 38   *Murō Saisei: Three Works*, translated by James O'Brien

No. 40   *Land of Volcanic Ash: A Play in Two Parts by Kubo Sakae*, translated by David G. Goodman

No. 41   *The Dreams of Our Generation and Selections from Beijing's People*, by Zhang Xinxin, edited and translated by Edward Gunn, Donna Jung and Patricia Farr

No. 43   *Post-War Japanese Resource Policies and Strategies: The Case of Southeast Asia*, by Shoko Tanaka

No. 44 *Family Change and the Life Course in Japan*, by Susan Orpett Long

No. 45 *Regulatory Politics in Japan: The Case of Foreign Banking*, by Louis W. Pauly

No. 46 *Planning and Finance in China's Economic Reforms*, by Thomas P. Lyons and WANG Yan

No. 48 *Bungo Manual: Selected Reference Materials for Students of Classical Japanese*, by Helen Craig McCullough

No. 49 *Ankoku Butō: The Premodern and Postmodern Influences on the Dance of Utter Darkness*, by Susan Blakeley Klein

No. 50 *Twelve Plays of the Noh and Kyōgen Theaters*, edited by Karen Brazell

No. 51 *Five Plays by Kishida Kunio*, edited by David Goodman

No. 52 *Ode to Stone*, by Shirō Hara, translated by James Morita

No. 53 *Defending the Japanese State: Structures, Norms and the Political Responses to Terrorism and Violent Social Protest in the 1970s and 1980s*, by Peter J. Katzenstein and Yutaka Tsujinaka

No. 54 *Deathsong of the River: A Reader's Guide to the Chinese TV Series* Heshang, by Su Xiaokang and Wang Luxiang, translated by Richard W. Bodman and Pin P. Wan

No. 55 *Psychoanalysis in China: Literary Transformations, 1919-1949*, by Jingyuan Zhang

No. 56 *To Achieve Security and Wealth: The Qing Imperial State and the Economy, 1644-1911*, edited by Jane Kate Leonard and John R. Watt

No. 57 *Like a Knife: Ideology and Genre in Contemporary Chinese Popular Music*, by Andrew F. Jones

No. 58   *Japan's National Security: Structures, Norms and Policy Responses in a Changing World*, by Peter J. Katzenstein and Nobuo Okawara

No. 59   *The Role of Central Banking in China's Economic Reforms*, by Carsten Holz

No. 60   *Warrior Ghost Plays from the Japanese Noh Theater: Parallel Translations with Running Commentary*, by Chifumi Shimazaki

No. 61   *Women and Millenarian Protest in Meiji Japan: Deguchi Nao and Ōmotokyō*, by Emily Groszos Ooms

No. 62   *Transformation, Miracles, and Mischief: The Mountain Priest Plays of Kyōgen*, by Carolyn Anne Morley

No. 63   *Selected Poems of Kim Namjo*, translated by David R. McCann and Hyunjae Yee Sallee

No. 64   *From Yalta to Panmunjom: Truman's Diplomacy and the Four Powers, 1945-1953*, by HUA Qingzhao

No. 65   *Kitahara Hakushū: His Life and Poetry*, by Margaret Benton Fukasawa

No. 66   *Strange Tales from Strange Lands: Stories by Zheng Wanlong*, edited and with an introduction by Kam Louie

No. 67   *Backed Against the Sea*, by Wang Wen-hsing, translated by Edward Gunn

No. 68   *The Sound of My Waves: Selected Poems by Ko Un*, translated by Brother Anthony of Taizé and Young-Moo Kim

Han Sŏrya and North Korean Literature, by Brian Myers, forthcoming winter 1993

For ordering information, please contact the Cornell East Asia Series, East Asia Program, Cornell University, 140 Uris Hall, Ithaca, NY 14853-7601, USA, (607) 255-6222.